Roger Davenport

■SCHOLASTIC

Point Horror has mutated...

Night of the Toxic Slime
Anthony Masters

Dissolvers
Andrew Matthews

Carnival of the Dead
Laurence Staig

coming soon...

Crawlers
Andrew Matthews

Scholastic Children's Books,
Commonwealth House, 1–19 New Oxford Street,
London WC1A 1NU, UK
a division of Scholastic Ltd
London ~ New York ~ Toronto ~ Sydney ~ Auckland
Mexico City ~ New Delhi ~ Hong Kong

First published in the UK by Scholastic Ltd, 2000

Copyright © Roger Davenport, 2000

ISBN 0 439 99637 6

Typeset by TW Typesetting, Midsomer Norton, Somerset
Printed by Cox & Wyman Ltd, Reading, Berks.

10 9 8 7 6 5 4 3 2 1

1

It was hot and bright again. When you stepped out of your front door you were prepared for the glare, your eyes already narrowed to a squint.

The weather caused quite a lot of comment in the small Midlands town. Was in fact the main topic of conversation. People said to each other in the street, "Never been an Autumn like it!" Or they might say, "A real Indian Summer, isn't it?" before they passed on their way slowly, savouring the sunshine, caught in the spell of a pleasant holiday-like lassitude.

In the Higgins' house they kept the curtains closed until dusk as a rule. "Too hot for me," Oona Higgins would say contentedly from the sofa, "with my migraines. But I'm not complaining!"

By happy chance, the unseasonably sunny weather coincided with a period of comparative idleness for every member of the family. Stuart Higgins was between jobs and it had been decided that daughter Kate should take a Gap Year to get her allergies sorted out. Time enough to put their shoulders to the wheel when they moved to their new life on the South coast.

The dyslexic of the family, Jake, had left school early. Stuart, his father, said in his broad Scots accent, "Eh, but a bright wee chap like you – you'll never be short of a pound or two." Stuart was like that; dryly cheerful, a good father, just as Oona was a good mother. While they had Scottish parents, Kate and Jake had been born in England and their Southern English accents did not quite match because Jake had been adopted at the age of five. "You fitted in straight away – no trouble at all!" Oona would say.

He still fitted in; was fond of his family. The Higgins were not well-off but they had each other, and it was enough. "You can't buy what we have," Stuart had once pronounced, "All the money in the world can't buy contentment." His pitted and pocked face creased into a complacent smile and dear, plump Oona nodded her agreement, her sad Celtic eyes glowing with serenity as she adjusted the neckline of her cheap baggy dress as though she were a Countess absently fingering priceless pearls.

Just for a moment or two Jake was discontented this afternoon. Still squinting against the light, he was kicking a football about on the recreation strip beside the police station, slamming it up against the side of the station itself. No one minded, it was all very easy-going here. Easy-going … and dull. He had quite a while to wait before his best mate, Billy Smith, would be free. Lunchtimes, when it was busy, Billy manned the shop counter in the little sub-post office just down the road, under the wan scrutiny of his mother.

Ah yes – that would kill a minute or two – he'd go and gloat. Billy loved football so much he was jealous of his friend's freedom to practise whenever he wanted to.

Jake came out through the gate in the high mesh-wire fence. They lived right on the outskirts of the town in a straggling no man's land of dwellings and businesses; to his right the road ascended steeply into open country past the local police station and the electricity pylon that towered upwards into the sky. Its massive base was enclosed by a spear-tipped steel fence on which a small red notice said, "*Keep Out. Danger of Death.*" Jake's reading was good enough for that, as it was for the enormous hoarding across the road from the pylon, which caught your eye with a friendlier legend: STOP AND SHOP: TAYLOR'S FRESH COUNTRY PRODUCE.

The sign referred to the market garden which stretched all the way down that side of the road, a narrow line of glasshouses which dazzled almost painfully in the sunshine.

His way led downhill past the yellow brick bus shelter, and in no time he was passing more yellow brickwork: that belonging to the house of the Higgins' neighbours, the ghastly Mr and Mrs Barton. Small and modern, the house was the double of his own next door, which in turn stood beside the post office. Across the street there were no houses at all, for where the greenhouses ended the flour factory began, blocking out the view down into the town proper because its dark red brick formed an "L" shape that continued around the bend in the road. Directly opposite the delivery yard in front of the factory was the doctor's surgery. Tremendous luck, to have a good doctor situated right on the Higgins' doorstep. Jake's sister, Kate, was there now for another consultation about her allergies.

So, all in all, it didn't take much time or energy to walk down to the post office.

Inside, the comparative gloom gave relief to the eyes. Billy's narrow face twitched into a smile of welcome as he nodded a hello from behind the shop counter. At once he had to sweep back his hair, which had fallen over his eyes. It was phenomenally fair and fine: his best feature, Kate had commented.

Other than his hair, she herself found little to like about Billy. Those pale blue eyes lacked warmth.

As for Jake, his liking for Billy was one of geographical necessity since there were in the neighbourhood no other youths of his own age and Jake was sociable by nature. There was, too, the matter of the superb games console Billy owned. The quality of his friend's possessions was way above anything Jake might hope for. Like the designer label tracksuit top he wore come rain or come shine. Was it because Billy came from a single-parent family that his mum gave in to his demands? Jake didn't know much about his family background. When he spoke, as he did now, his voice was cultured, although the words were colloquial.

"How you going, Jake?"

"Good, thanks…"

"How's Kate?"

"Oh – good, thanks." Jake had an idea that Billy fancied his sister and wasn't sure what he felt about it.

"She should come round and do video games or something, sometime."

"She's not into that."

Jake leaned against the shop-counter, football under his arm, and they fell silent, easy in each other's company after long acquaintance.

There was one other customer in the shop; a

factory worker in grey overalls. He had his back to them, browsing the video tapes up by the post-office section.

"Any new tapes in?" Jake enquired at last, for something to say. He was smaller than Billy, stocky and dark. Like a superball, his mother said, all pent-up energy.

"No – not yet," Billy sighed.

At the moment both of them were without regular television because their houses were on cable and there was some frustrating local fault with the system.

"Well, tell your mum to get some. Tell her she's running an entertainment service here and if she doesn't get new videos in she'll have to come round and sing to us instead."

It was an unlikely idea, if you knew Mrs Smith. She was old before her time, grey-faced and listless. Billy smiled his short smile again to acknowledge a joke had been made.

Jake had one of his periods of rapid, disorganized thought. *We could go to the movies if we had some money. Why do we always talk about going to the cinema and never go? I bet I could get a job if I tried. I hope Kate's all right. Why does every day have to be just the same as the last one?*

And then, within the space of a few seconds, the day wasn't the same as the ones which had gone before.

The factory worker was coughing. His back was to them and his head was down as he examined a video-tape box. It was comical, listening to him trying to clear his throat with progressively loud hawking. Jake caught Billy's eye and they smiled at the man's discomfort.

The man bent over and coughed some more. Then he swung round, doubled up and retched. And spewed. Quantities of some grey liquid gushed from his wide open mouth in huge, irregular gouts. It was as if he were regurgitating wallpaper paste, enough to cover the Great Wall of China. It splashed down his overalls and pooled on the floor. There were black streaks among the grey. He slipped and fell face forward into the mess he had produced. His body heaved and twitched and he began to scream.

Jake was shocked into stillness and it was Billy who began to shout for help and it was Billy who went to the man's side, kneeling in the grey-black stickiness to turn the factory worker's head to one side so that he could breathe.

The post office filled up pretty quickly. Fellow-factory-workers in their overalls; the ghastly Mrs Barton, agog, clutching some knitting. Permanently pop-eyed and red-faced, her fascination with this scene was definitely that of the semi-professional voyeur. No one seemed to know what to do until Billy's mother came out from the back of the shop.

Mrs Smith did not seem as shocked as everyone else. "The surgery's only next door," she said with dull patience.

Two of the men picked up the sick worker, who must by this time have been emptied of all liquid matter. The noise he was making now was a dry one, anyway, a whistling breath like a badly-tuned radio, high-pitched and alarming. He was a big man and because his body was becoming convulsed in violent spasms they had difficulty lifting him and carrying him out through the door. The little crowd made it no easier by pressing in to look more closely at his ashen face.

It appeared that everyone was in a state of shock. "Must be the weather," one co-worker said, and hesitated. "Pleasant morning."

"Lovely," another murmured.

"We need the rain, though." Mrs Burton remarked to no one in particular.

Standing there, she had begun to knit.

It was odd.

When the shop had emptied Jake helped Billy clear up the mess. The grey goo was hard to shift and it took a long time. When the floor was finally sluiced clean Mrs Smith said to Jake, wearily, "You're a good boy, Jake. That's a real help."

"We could have a kick-about now," Billy said keenly. "That's all right, isn't it, Mum?"

"No. Don't feel like it." Jake was surprised at how

calm Billy had remained. "D'you think he'll be all right? What was it?"

Billy shrugged. "Could've been anything. How would I know? What about a video game, then?"

"No. Got to get back. See you later."

"You're a good boy, Jake," Mrs Smith repeated from behind the grille.

Their dad was out with Uncle Jimmy, learning his new trade as a plumber, and one of Oona's migraines had sent her upstairs to lie down. When Jake came downstairs after visiting her on her sickbed the house felt empty and he found himself missing his family. Ludicrous, when you knew they were all so close by and would soon be together again. Yet they were a family who loved each other – and who told each other so at every opportunity. In case they ever forgot, in the hall the only picture was a framed embroidery of red words on a green background: "Home is where the heart is."

Jake's learning difficulties intervened here. He had always read it as "Home is the place where the *heat* is," without ever questioning the sense of such a slogan.

Kate came back from the doctor's with a new puffer for her hay-fever. Because he loved her so much he felt a wave of relief when she said blithely, "Waste of time," and went to put the kettle on.

When he got his cup of tea Jake said, "Thanks.

Love you," and she responded with the automatic "Love you too."

He told her about the drama in the post office, ending with, "There was something really weird about it…"

She was reading one of her women's magazines at the kitchen table. Kate was green-eyed, with freckles and thick auburn hair. They could hardly have looked less alike.

She flicked over a page with impatient boredom. Kate had this fascination with babies at the moment and read articles with teasing titles like, *"Helpless in the face of wind"*.

"Oh, look at that one," she said warmly, turning the magazine in Jake's direction.

Jake feigned surprise. "Oh – a baby!"

"He's so sweet."

"Anyway – it wasn't very nice. And then the things people said…"

"What things?" She wasn't interested. She was going on to the letters page. *"The Well-Baby Clinic saw us through!"*

"Well … it didn't fit what was going on. Just so strange."

"Why?"

"They talked about the weather."

"What's wrong with that?"

"Well, I mean, he could have been dying. There was something weird about it…"

Kate was a wondrously placid girl usually. Now she got cross. "Oh don't be so stupid." She got up and went to the kitchen radio. When she turned it on the disc jockey sprang straight into life with one of his catchphrases, "And what do we think about that one? If you ask me, it's Awwl RIGHT!"

"See?" Kate said. "Says it all!"

Uncle Jimmy stayed for supper, as he often did. It was a simple meal of sausages and chips; a happy occasion, like all the mealtimes in the Higgins' house.

"Och, yes – I heard about the fella in the post office." Jimmy shook his head ruefully, making his grey ponytail swing heavily from side to side. "You know what it was?"

"No," Jake said. Uncle Jimmy smiled at him and took another mouthful of food, teasing, putting off the moment when he relieved Jake's curiosity.

"Epilepsy," he said indistinctly.

"What?"

"Epilepsy – and serious too." Uncle Jimmy looked serious himself for a moment. Usually he had this half-smile on his face, a twitch of reckless amusement. "It can come on sudden like that, they say, without any warning."

"See?" said Stuart Higgins, after a solemn pause, "We have to be grateful for what we have. You never know what's round the corner."

This drew Jake on to another subject that was

occupying his mind. "The trouble is – we do. We know exactly what each day's going to be like before it's started – it's going to be like every other day round here."

"What d'you mean, son?" asked Uncle Jimmy gently. He wasn't a real relative; he was Stuart's oldest friend, another Scot. When things went against you, there was Uncle Jimmy on the doorstep, with sympathy or – better yet – a plan. Like the plan he had come up with to get Stuart back to work with a chance of decent money. He was around fifty and the ponytail did not look out of place because he had this audacious, piratical quality about him.

Jake looked at his food. "I know we've got all we need and everything. But we never *do* anything."

"Aha," said Uncle Jimmy at once. "Time for a picnic. How about that idea – eh?"

Ignoring this, Jake said, "It wasn't right – what happened with that man."

This time it was his father who was angry. "Oh – leave it! Banging on about something that's got nothing to do with us!"

His bad temper did not last. After supper they went into the front room for a game of Racing Demon. The Higgins played cards every night – it was a family ritual and very loud and cheerful.

"Sorry!" said Stuart, slamming down a card just before Kate could get hers down, "Had to do it!"

"Of course you did. Love you, Dad."

"Love you."

It was round about here that Jimmy finished his cup of tea and said his farewells and left on his motorbike. Jake had a suspicion that all the lovey-dovey stuff got under his skin too.

Later they all sat together and watched one of the videos they had hired from the post office. They got almost everything they needed at the post office, allowing Jimmy to bring in anything more exotic from town.

The video was a wildlife documentary, showing how swans bonded together and cared for their young.

Then it was time for hot chocolate: the last ritual of the day. A warm time with a warm drink and loving goodnights and kisses exchanged all round.

" 'Night Mum."

"Oh darling wee boy ... night–night. And you, lovely Kate."

"Love you."

"Love you."

"See you in the morning."

That night there was another peculiar occurrence. Jake had been asleep in the half of the back bedroom that belonged to him. Jack of all trades, Uncle Jimmy had fixed up a short plaster-board partition like a screen "so Kate can have a little privacy – which she needs at her age." In friendly style, the beds were arranged smack on either side of the plasterboard, allowing intimate conversation between brother and sister.

A change in his environment woke Jake in the early hours. Light was coming in through the window, growing by the second. All at once the whole room was shot through with an eerie effulgence like an electric storm.

"Kate?" Jake whispered once, and let her sleep on. He threw back the duvet and got out of bed and as he did so the light vanished from the sky. He went anyway to the window, which was open. The curtains were too, because with these hot nights you felt cooler that way.

A peek round the end of the partition: Kate was comfortably insensible, formless under her covers. He turned his attention back to the window. Across their back yard, across the narrow strip of intervening wasteland, the grey four-storey council-flat building showed a single square of light from behind an unpatterned blind drawn down over a second-floor window. There was always someone awake somewhere in the flats.

It seemed that no one else had been made curious by the unexpected brightening of the sky. The windows of the flats remained dark and the one lit blind stayed down.

Jake stayed there for quite a time, breathing in the stale air of a still night. He stayed until the rain came and then he went back to bed, lulled to drowsiness by the continuous noise it made. It fell in a heavy downpour that lasted only a couple of minutes, a fusillade of water bullets that ricocheted off the concrete paving of the yard and rattled the guttering.

All quite normal. The swans had seen out a storm like that under a willow tree, in the documentary.

When the rain had subsided, soft gurglings came from the down-pipe on the outer wall, stroking the recent drama away.

"A summer storm," Jake thought to himself sleepily. Nothing odd. A late summer storm. Thunder and lightning and rain.

Only … what was it? Something missing. What?

There had been no thunder.

The next day was hot and bright with a faint vapour in the air following the storm. Life went on as normal. Just as normal. In the morning Jimmy stopped by on his motorcycle to give Stuart a lift down into town to study plumbing and, just as the sounds of the bike's engine had faded to nothing, their neighbours' door slammed and out came Mr Barton to squeeze his loose, flabby bulk into his quaint old three-wheeler car. About an hour after he had puttered uphill out of town, Mrs Barton would plant her staring face in their front window and begin her day's knitting. What it was she made it was never possible to tell, but by her work-rate you guessed she had a lot of them.

Kate and Jake had their morning hot chocolate

watching a video. *It's a Wonderful Life* was a good film in its way, showing a good man loved by his family and all around him, but they had seen it before and it was in black and white and, as usual, the video recorder was occasionally uneven as it played. They liked sitting together, though. Jake felt loving and protective and when the cup of chocolate was drained he put his arm around Kate's shoulder and she snuggled into him. Life was good.

The bell rang. Kate said, "Regular or relief?"

"Regular."

"Relief. And if it is, you make the chocolate tonight."

It wasn't a chore, to do something for your family – to spare Kate her regular little duty. He said, "If it's the relief I'll be in charge of chocolate from now on – deal?"

"Hey now – you're on!"

He was already in the narrow hallway.

It was the relief postman at the door, a retired schoolteacher who was popular in the community. He was short and neat with an upper-upper class accent that went well with his hawklike nose; a man of about sixty with large grey eyes that looked out from under hooded eyelids that were almost transparent, so fine was the skin. You knew he'd been a teacher by his easy manner of command and he made Jake uncomfortable because he'd probably been up for hours and Jake was still in his pyjamas.

Now he made him more uncomfortable. "How's the reading coming along?"

"Oh – pretty good," Jake lied. Mr Roche had heard of his learning difficulties and had lent Jake a series of brightly coloured little-word books for little people. They were too shaming even to open.

"That's good. And everything going well?"

"Great, yeah."

"Your post, sir," Mr Roche said, acting like some kind of servant. The joke did not suit him.

One of the letters was an envelope too big to fit through the letterbox. The rest was junk mail. Mr Roche smiled as he handed it over. "Sorry – the best I could do."

"Oh, well – it's not your, erm … cup of tea?"

Because their house and the Bartons' marked the end of his delivery route, Mr Roche sometimes came in for a chat. Not today though. "No thanks – I'm promised to your neighbour today," he said and turned away into the dazzling light.

Later Oona opened the big envelope. It was a solicitor's letter about the house they were buying near Bournemouth. Jimmy was helping out there, otherwise, as Stuart said, it would have been, "No way, José". Oona was not at all a woman of business and put the letter aside rather rapidly, as though just by reading it she might enter into a contract she couldn't fulfil. She got on to a happier subject immediately. "Now then, Kate darling, and darling

Jake – it's all fixed and we're going to have a picnic. Now what about that?"

Both were enthusiastic. It seemed that Jimmy was giving Stuart the day off and was going to borrow a car. "Well, that's more like it!" Jake beamed.

Only it wasn't like it at all. Uncle Jimmy's deal with the car had fallen through, and there they all were with a bag full of goodies and no place to go.

Except… "There's always the Rec," said Uncle Jimmy brightly.

"Not exactly a beauty spot, is it?" Jake answered sarcastically.

But they had each other, and that was enough. And the recreation strip was deserted, so they had it all to themselves. "Lords of all we survey," Stuart said.

They surveyed the blank wall of the police station. They surveyed the van with the "Taylor's" logo on it, as it swept into sight coming down the hill and went on down into town. They surveyed their lunch and ate it with relish. And even Jake cheered up. He had a fast eating competition with Kate which made them both laugh and splutter. It was OK.

When Billy Smith turned up with his football it was even better, even if he did show off a lot for Kate's benefit. Jimmy joined in the kickabout and was kind enough to go in goal for a good half-hour.

The rest of the family, prompted by Oona's prediction of an on-coming migraine, went home, though in good spirits.

Leaving Billy to practise catching the ball between his neck and shoulder, Jimmy and Jake took a break, lying on the astroturf.

"It's a good life, eh, Jake?" said Jimmy.

"We're so lucky," Jake said sincerely.

"Got all you want already and there's more to come. Things couldn't be better."

"Yes. Only…"

"Only?"

"Oh, I don't know." Then he did know. "I think I'm going to take a walk up the hill."

Jimmy let a smile arrive on his face. "Get on with you, then."

Jake got up and walked out from the recreation area. Passing the police station he was suddenly nervous and looked in at a window. Behind the desk the sergeant raised a hand in greeting. Jake thought, *now that was silly. The police couldn't care less where I'm going.*"

Nearing the fence around the pylon the sign reminded him that there was Danger of Death.

He paused. As it did going the other way down into town, the road curved away beyond the pylon. Now he saw it, it was almost a right-angled turn, going around the police station. Had he ever walked past the pylon? He couldn't remember. Well, he would: right now. He took a determined pace forward and stopped immediately. He couldn't do it and he was feeling terribly anxious suddenly, wanting to go on and at the same time rationalizing an impulse to flight. It just wasn't worth it. Now, if the road had led straight out of town, well, that would be different, wouldn't it? You'd have a sense of getting somewhere.

Perhaps another time.

Half a minute later he was coming back through the gate into the recreation strip. "Yo, come on, then," he called to Billy, and the ball arrived at his feet.

Jimmy got up from where he'd been sitting. "You be careful boys. Don't want to get sunstroke." He stretched. "Ah well, that was good. Be seeing you."

It wasn't long before Billy and Jake quit their game and meandered home. One of the overalled factory workers was going into Taylor's greenhouses to fill up a box with fresh country produce. "'Lo, Billy. Turned out nice again. Lovely."

"Yeah," Billy answered and turned to Jake. "See you round, man."

"After tea?"

"Maybe," Billy shouted over his shoulder, already dribbling the ball down towards the post office.

Mrs Barton was visible in her window, knitting. Her heavily made-up lips wormed into a kind of smile as Jake looked in at her. He grinned back politely, with equal insincerity. Still, if he thought he didn't have an exciting life, what about her?

Indoors, Kate was listening to the small radio in the kitchen. She was thinking. More accurately, tuning in to the urges in her body. Children. In a cruel world, what was there nicer, more beautiful and more vulnerable than a young child? And yet it would be a battle of wits. She smiled to herself. As one of the baby books said, "The infant wants constant reassurance and can read the smallest signals sent out by Mum, who must be careful to show that he cannot have total dominance over her."

To have children you had to have a man. Men… Young men… She had not seen one yet that had the necessary qualities to be the father of her precious child. They never saw anyone, here. She sighed. Maybe in their new home… Maybe the boy next door would be a bit like Jake, a boy who could make you laugh and who wanted to look after you like Jake did. Not that she fancied him or anything, because he was her brother, but he was certainly the only young male she thought anything of.

And now here he was, swinging into the kitchen with that look of someone who wanted action and couldn't find any. *Men*… On the radio that local disc jockey was saying, "It's awwwl RIGHT" and it was now Jake was here.

"Yo, Kate. That was OK, wasn't it? Worked out quite well in the end."

"It was lovely. Oh – Jake…"

"Mmm?" He had gone straight to the bread bin, on the understanding that he was always hungry even when he didn't know it.

"The surgery phoned – said could you pop in because your next appointment's got squeezed out by something urgent. They could see you at five, they said."

"It's a waste of time," Jake said, not caring one way or another. It would at least be something to do, to go and sit in the chair and let Dr Dunning fiddle with the coloured specs he was trying in order to combat Jake's dyslexia. None of the Higgins' minded going to the doctor, although it had to be said that Dr Dunning was not the most sympathetic man you could meet. Good at his job though and nothing was too much trouble for him. Not Oona's migraines or Stuart's blood pressure – he always made time for them all. Conscientious to a fault.

Now Jake had the soft white slice of bread in his hand he didn't want it. His stomach was hurting: he must have eaten too fast at the picnic.

Dr Dunning's surgery had endless piped music, the synthetic kind where you couldn't tell what kind of instruments were meant to be playing. Jake sat in the waiting room with a man from the factory and a young woman with a distinct hunch and an unhappy face. An older woman came from the surgery with a prescription and went to the reception desk. "I've been reduced," she said apathetically.

The receptionist was a large young woman who said carefully, "Well, lucky you. I wish I could be."

"Ha ha," they both went and the older woman left.

The tannoy speaker cleared its throat with a blip. "Jake Higgins," it requested.

The surgery was larger than the waiting room and as clean and antiseptic as the doctor himself. He was fifty or thereabouts, white-coated and tall and he had a long face which needed two shaves a day. His eyes were set so deep in his skull that you imagined he would never need sunglasses because light would never reach them. Dark they were; so black that it was impossible to differentiate the pupils from the cornea. When he spoke you had the impression he could have been talking to an imaginary friend he didn't much care for, since there was no spark of life in the way he spoke. Jake knew he was supposed to like him, and couldn't.

"In the chair…" the doctor murmured. "We'll try some… I've got some new lenses."

Jake settled back in the divan-style chair and Dr Dunning put spectacles on his nose. "One green, one blue. Look at the chart, would you."

Jake looked at the eye-test chart. Dr Dunning came back into view with another chart he hung over the first. It had proper sentences on it.

"And how's things?"

"Fine," said Jake.

"All well with the family?"

"Yup."

"Take a look at that first phrase."

"'The leaves are green,'" Jake read out, bored already and feeling strangely sleepy.

"It was all that sun. You shouldn't have run around so much."

Oona was clucking over Jake, the anxious mother. On his way back from Dr Dunning Jake's stomach had complained with such force that he almost doubled over.

"And you ate so fast. It's not polite, apart from anything else."

"I'm all right, Mum. I'm just not hungry, that's all."

And he was so incredibly tired, too. Sometimes it was like that after he'd been to the doctor.

Life went on as normal all the same. He wouldn't forego the evening fun, a family game of poker tonight, suggested by Stuart. They used scraps of paper as chips and pretended they were worth millions. Oona was hopeless and Kate didn't care, which meant that on the last hand only the men were left in the game. They were playing draw poker and by a magnificent coincidence Jake built up an unbeatable Royal Flush.

Stuart liked to appear tough when they played poker. As the betting rose he said with a touch of a sneer, "Give it up, son. You've no more got a decent hand than I've got bubonic plague."

Jake had him, he had him. "Put your money where your mouth is, then."

Kate raised her eyebrows at that. They were never confrontational, the Higgins'.

Stuart's tough act began to look all too real. "You want it – you've got it. This is for the lot – right here and now. That OK by you?"

He couldn't resist it: Jake let a flicker of fake doubt show. Then said, "Sure – fine by me."

"Oh, God, son – you'll never make a card player." Stuart turned over his hand. "See? Full house! Beat that."

In answer Jake laid out his hand one card at a time.

Stuart's face went dead. There was no other word for it. As a displacement activity he took the rest of the cards from Kate and shuffled them, looking the while at Jake's hand laid out in all its glory. At last he said hoarsely, "Well done, son."

It cost him. Kate grimaced "oops" at Jake while Oona sat there with a look of uncomprehending worry. Above them the ornate brass light fitting clicked a couple of times, as it was wont to do. It made Jake aware of the silence in the room. Clearly it would be injudicious to do a war-dance of delight right here and now, but he was going to savour his triumph somewhere. He got up. "I'll make the chocolate, shall I?"

His back was towards them and he was grinning all the way into the kitchen, restored to full vigour.

However, while doling out the spoonfuls of the heavy brown powder his stomach reminded him of the insults done to it earlier and he had the unthinkable thought that maybe he'd skip the ritual drink tonight. Or maybe have something else instead.

When he carried the tray into the front room again Oona was on the sofa with Stuart, whose head Kate was massaging. Oona was giggling. "It's me that has the headaches – not you!"

"Aye, well…" Stuart mumbled. He looked drawn and tired and discouraged. Glancing up at Jake, he flushed, displaying a residue of anger. "Took your time, didn't you?"

Who'd have thought he could be such a poor loser? Jake set the tray down on the coffee table and picked up his own cup at once, going to the one armchair. He wondered if anyone could smell from the sofa how very much tastier than theirs his drink was.

It was made with real chocolate. He'd taken longer than usual because he'd grated it from a bar and it had come out so superior to that other muck.

Later complete harmony reigned again and there was the customary dialogue at bedtime.

"Love you."

"Love you."

"See you in the morning, I love you."

He didn't sleep for a long time. His stomach was OK now; it was only he felt so awake. When he did at last drift off he dreamed the birthday dream. It never varied and he thought he dreamed it so he could better appreciate the gift of family life that had been granted him when, at the age of five, he had been adopted by Stuart and Oona. As always in the dream, the orphanage dining hall was dark, lit only by the candles on his cake. Children's faces smiled or looked envious in the surrounding shadows. He felt embarrassed at having to blow the candles out in front of such a large assembly, but he leaned over and in one sweeping breath extinguished all the light there was.

As happened every time, the absence of light gave cause for dream-worry: out of the blackness something bad was bound to come, would be here soon... When the anxiety reached a high pitch, he woke.

His mind was instantly clear. There was something wrong with that dream. What?

The faces clustered round.

His happiness.

The cake.

Which had ten candles.

3

He was still thinking about it as he played head tennis with Billy on the Rec. Such a small thing and so easily explained, yet it bothered him. Ten candles, there had been. Four going down in a straight line, making a one, and six in a straggling oval, making a zero. The number ten. He was sure that was the way he always dreamed it.

Billy simply never tired of football. Now they were doing chestings down and it went on and on. Were all Jake's friends so single-minded? Funny – he'd already forgotten so much about his old school, and he'd only just left. He could picture a couple of guys, hazily, and there was his arch-enemy, Mr Edward, the DT teacher, prematurely bald and small and dour, but the rest of it…

Well there you go. Life moves on.

The mini bus went by with its silent passengers looking straight ahead. Ten candles in the orphanage. When his last birthday there had been his fifth.

"And one-on-one. Let's get it on," Billy panted.

"No." Jake wasn't as good as he was and his heart wasn't in it and he'd had enough.

"Why not?"

"Fed up with it."

"Why? Something I've done?"

"No. I'm, um… I think I'll go home, see what Kate's up to."

"Just see if you can get past me. Bet you can't."

"I don't care, Billy. I'm going home."

Billy looked hurt.

So what. What a dump this place was.

Two women stood outside the Taylor's greenhouses. One said laboriously, "I said to her, I said, 'It's the hottest on record.'"

"Yes," the other woman said, "That's what they say, isn't it?"

It was all they said round here.

Oona was making an apple pie, while Stuart was having trouble staying awake after a visit to the surgery. Dr Dunning had given him new pills for his blood pressure and they had a sedative effect. Up in her part of their room Kate was making notes on natural childbirth. Useless to talk to her when she was caught up with that, so he gave her a kiss and went round to his part of the room and fell on the bed with maximum weight.

Oof. What a dump.

Ten candles.

Oona's pie was their pudding that night. It was burnt and very crumbly. "I don't know what went wrong," Oona said brightly. "I'm usually a good cook." This was so far from being the truth that no one even bothered to make a joke about it.

Keeping to the new roster he had agreed with Kate, Jake made the bedtime drink, as he had the night before. Again he made his own with real chocolate and the taste was sensational.

"Love you love you good night." Another day done.

Jake wondered if he'd have the dream. Tried to make his mind a blank so's he'd drop off sooner. The orphanage did not surface from his subconscious; instead he got flashes of Dr Dunning, from their last encounter: fragments of a conversation he had not recalled having.

"So, Jake. What's it like sharing a bedroom with your sister?"

"It's good."

"And how do you feel about her?"

"Well, I love her. She's my sister."

"Yes, so you like to be close to her."

"Yes."

"You feel protective towards her."

"Yes. I don't know what I'd do if anything happened to her."

He recollected Dr Dunning's face coming closer as he leaned forward to fix him with those deep-set eyes. *"And supposing she was in terrible danger? What would you do then?"*

"I'd try to save her – I'd do anything to save her."

"You would, wouldn't you. And you're getting on all right with your parents? Nothing about them that disturbs you?"

"No. What do you mean?"

"Nothing. I'm happy if you're happy."

"I'm happy."

That was it. What had happened after that? He couldn't bring anything else to mind. How funny.

Jake sat up in bed with vague and restless urgings gnawing at his gut. There was no chance of sleeping for ages. What to do. Read? Huh. More like work than pleasure. He looked at his watch. Only ten o'clock. They all went to bed very early in his house, didn't they?

Well, Billy didn't. He always boasted about how he got extra life because he slept so little. There was a good idea. Sneak round and have a word with Billy. About…?

About how things didn't seem quite right here. He wanted to make up with Billy anyway after that small row they'd had. Billy was dead intelligent. Jake would see which way the conversation was going and if it looked like there was a natural opening he'd just say, casually, something like, "Know something funny? A couple of days ago I wanted to walk up the hill and I couldn't. Anything like that ever happen to you?"

He got dressed in the dark. Looked out of the window. There were the flats, with only a couple of lights on, as usual. It seemed other people went to bed early round here, too. He could climb the garden fence: the post office was only next door and most of it was Billy's home – and there was a smudge of yellow light coming from their kitchen. Good. He was smiling to himself as he went cautiously downstairs. This was more like living.

The door to the front room was slightly ajar and a lamp was on. Jake looked through the crack. Oona was in there on the sofa with a romantic novel and, by the look on her face, another headache. Poor Mum. He turned and went down the tiny hall into the kitchen, where he felt his way along the units to the paler patch of light that marked the kitchen door. The key was in the lock and the bolts worked easily. He went out into the garden, his trainers making no noise on the concrete crazy paving. It was less dark out here than indoors and the air was warm and still; the shrubs and plants in the narrow borders looked dry and dispirited.

It was the silence that got to him. It might as well

have been three in the morning rather than two hours before midnight. The wooden fence that looked so sturdy was disconcertingly flexible. The only way to get over without making too much noise was to get in tight to it and haul oneself up as when doing a chin-up and continue upwards till one's arms were straight and juddering as they pressed down on the top of the fence. Lever the right leg up and… Now he was straddling the fence and it was making protesting sounds and this wasn't working right at all. Well, if he couldn't be quiet he'd be quick. He flipped his other leg over and pushed off and jumped down on to paving just like that in his own garden. Immediately he could see through the panes in the back door that Billy was in there and that he was alone. Jake nearly started laughing. This was so good. He'd give him a spooky surprise.

The reason he'd not been heard climbing the fence was at once clear. Billy had his back to him and was watching a TV set up on a bracket in the corner of the room. From a safe distance of about three metres from the door, Jake watched as well. It was a film, and an excellent one too. Spider-like aliens had invaded New York and, by the look of it, the hero and heroine were trapped in a sewer full of them, trying to set up a bomb that would destroy the nest.

Which of course they did. There was then a scene of solemn congratulations from the military and some men in suits and a fade-out on a kiss. Enjoying his secrecy, Jake watched it all. Perhaps he wouldn't alert Billy to his presence: would instead baffle him the next day by knowing what he had watched. He must get Billy to lend him that tape. He'd not seen it in the post office.

The moment the credits rolled Billy used the remote to put the set on standby and switched off the video. Jake spied on, just to see if there would be anything else he could tease him with in the morning. It would be nothing too dramatic, that looked certain, as Billy went to cupboards and drawers and got out a mixing bowl, a wooden spoon and a bag of flour. Was he going to make a pie, like Oona? If he was, then he definitely had talents he'd never spoken of.

Billy fetched a bowl of sugar and a pitcher of water and a sieve and set them, too, on the table. He poured half the bag of flour into the sieve and pounded it through into the bowl with the spoon, adding judicious quantities of sugar and water to the mix. Growing bored with the process, just as Jake did when he was making his chocolate, he dumped the rest of the flour into the mixing bowl, followed it with a heap of sugar, splashed in more water and pounded away.

The result was a white lumpy mess submerged in a lake of cloudy water. Billy was going to cook that?

No. He was going to eat it.

Jake watched in wonder and disgust. Billy ate as if

his life depended on it, spooning up great gobs of the stuff and ramming into his mouth. *Well, I'll definitely mention this in the morning*, Jake thought. As he ate, Billy speeded up into a kind of animal excess, slopping in the mixture at a tremendous rate. Jake had not noticed before how wide his mouth could open.

At last he was done. The bowl was empty.

Not for long. Billy sat back, his face smeared all over with the delicacy he had prepared so carelessly. He yawned widely and put his head back. It twitched from side to side in a quick mechanical kind of way and then he bucked forward with his head lolling over the bowl and spewed and spewed, vomiting back all he had eaten in irregular, loose projectiles.

Jake now thought it wouldn't be something he would talk about. Instead, should he knock on the door right now? Surely Billy had epilepsy, like the man in the post office – he was ill.

He didn't look ill. Lifting his head at last he seemed to be looking straight at Jake, with a sleepy, self-satisfied smile. Eschewing use of the spoon this time, he raised the bowl and drank deeply.

When the liquid content of the bowl had disappeared down his throat he ate the more solid matter with the spoon.

Jake stood there. It couldn't get any worse now.

It did. His hunger satisfied, twice, Billy bounced

out of his chair and went to the TV set. Reaching up, he opened the control flap and pressed buttons. The set came to life with a resolution of far less quality than before and with a content that was static in the extreme. It was a wide-angle view from the ceiling of Jake's own front room. There was Oona, sprawled on the sofa with her book. The picture was dim and grainy. Jake saw Oona lick a finger, turn a page, and read on.

Physically nothing happened anywhere. Billy looked at the screen; Jake stood in the dark garden; Oona read her novel.

In Jake's head a lot was happening. It was expressed inadequately in mental words.

This is bad.

And there was the silence. How in heaven's name could he climb the fence now, with the noise that made. If there was one thing clear in his mind it was that Billy Smith should never know he was here; should never find out he had been in the garden tonight, watching.

He wanted out, and fast. Billy turned from the television and Jake's nerves were such that he involuntarily took a step backwards. His foot met an empty plastic plant tub. It toppled and rolled. He grabbed it and set it upright at once. The noise had been small, yet Billy was looking this way. He could only see the glass in the window, reflecting the kitchen light, but there was a listening, alert cast to his expression. *He might think it's a cat*, Jake thought frantically. And then thought, *There are no cats in this town. I've never seen one*, and turned and ran. The thick rubber soles of his trainers met the concrete lightly, almost soundlessly; he had only fifteen metres to go until he reached the end wall, which was brick and ran all the way from the post office to Mr and Mrs Barton's house and beyond.

How do you climb a six foot brick wall when in the grip of terror? You throw yourself straight at it and let instinct do the rest. His hands clutched the top of the wall, both feet scrabbled against it, and then he was vaulting over in a flying somersault.

He landed on his back on hard earth with an impact that winded him. He could neither breathe nor move for several seconds. But he listened for footsteps. And heard … nothing. The silence was absolute except for a far-off thumping in his head until he was able to drag air back into his lungs, and that sounded like a whole army gasping for breath.

Even at this distance he could hear Billy's kitchen door open.

And he could hear it shut, too, only a few moments later.

Safe.

Safe?

After a while he got up into a crouching position and remained there until the light went off in Billy's kitchen. Then he ran along the waste ground, bent over way below the level of the wall, until he was sure he was at the back of his own house.

The base of his spine was aching from the fall. He climbed the wall with shaking arms and dropped down on to home territory.

The light was still on in the living room. He sneaked past and up the stairs with no thought of going in, nor of speaking to his mother.

Still dressed, he lay on his bed. Here was his own place, his familiar space where nothing could happen to him. The part of their family home that was his alone.

It didn't feel like being at home at all. Things were different now.

Sunlight through the curtains and the warmth of the morning brought no feeling of a return to normality. It was normality itself that was in question. In the long hours before sleep finally seeped into him like a drug that would not be denied, he had gone over and over his circumstances in a futile attempt to make some kind of sense of them. There was a similarity in Billy's newly-discovered eating habits and in the illness of the factory worker in the post office. This similarity raised further questions about the men and women who lived here. When he was younger Jake had indulged himself in the popular fantasy that he might be one of a kind – that others around him were keeping this secret from him: that he was so special as to be unique. When it could be happening in actuality, you found you didn't want to be unique. You wanted to be one of a species, cosy within some happy subset such as a crowd of partisan football supporters... Or a happy family.

What was it Dr Dunning had asked about his parents – if Jake remembered their talk rightly?

"Nothing about them that disturbs you?"

But he loved them. They were his mum and dad. And what about Kate? He found he worried for Kate more than himself, and his worry was, *I mustn't worry Kate*. It was all so confusing.

His eyes and lids were raw with fatigue. There were strange people around him and he and his family were being observed. His best friend was in all probability no friend at all. What he had to do today was to go on just as usual and keep on the look-out. That had been his last conscious thought last night and it was his resolve now as he dressed and prepared to be ... normal.

What the hell would he *say* when he saw Billy?

In the event there was a lot to think about before he and Billy Smith met up on the recreation strip.

He was in a quandary as he heated the milk in the morning. So far he'd managed to make his own drink on his own in the kitchen; today everyone was in here, including Uncle Jimmy, who came to stand beside him as he spooned out the powdered chocolate.

"Grand way to start the day," Jimmy nodded approvingly. "Sets you up great."

"Yes… D'you want some?"

"Ah … no – nothing sweet for me."

Just to drive him from his side Jake insisted, "Go on – try some."

It worked. "No no. I'll pass, thanks." Jimmy went to Stuart. "Another fine day and we're going to be stuck inside, working…!"

But he did eat sweet things. And he had sugar in his tea, too. With just one cup to go, his own, Jake mimed putting in the chocolate, with his back to the others; then poured in the warm milk for real. He gave everyone else their mugs and went back to his. He wanted to drink it quickly, but the milk on its own was too hot and brought sweat to his brow. Talk about Billy Smith being different than he'd thought – he himself, Jake, had been different since he'd stopped taking the chocolate. He'd been livelier, with much more get up and go without the soothing family drink. The hot chocolate twice a day without fail…

The chocolate Uncle Jimmy brought them from town. Uncle Jimmy, who had sat and watched as Jake walked to the edge of town, and who had left the moment Jake was back; and then, when Jake got home … well. This was a step without foundation maybe, but he'd been sent straight to Dr Dunning, who did so little for his dyslexia.

His heart began to work faster and a little adrenalin rush prepared him for unspecified danger. He managed to finish the hot milk and rinsed the mug straight away. Was there a way he could wean Kate off the chocolate – perhaps without her knowledge? He looked over at her, serene and dreamy, leaning against the kitchen units and sipping the drink. Whatever it was that was happening round here, he desired above all else that she be safe.

And that meant finding out more. Which in turn meant that he would speak to no one, not even Kate, in case his new knowledge reached a wider public.

How simple it is to dissemble; how naturally it comes when the need is there. In the afternoon kickabout with Billy it was easy to go on as if nothing had changed, after a deep breath as you saw him coming along to join you. You just let yourself remember what every other day had been like and everything fell into place. Meanwhile the mind worked independently of the body.

When do I see Dr Dunning next? If we talk and I don't remember it, then it looks like he gets me to tell him stuff... Look at that bloke eating his packed lunch by the bus stop... Is he watching us playing football? Or is he watching me?

The greenhouse worker outside Taylor's wasn't watching him, anyway. The man was unrolling turf to renew the green strip that ran along the side of the nursery. Every time Jake glanced over he was clearly concentrating on his work. Jake trapped the ball on his thigh and passed it back to Billy in one fluid move. It was funny, but his football skills were improved remarkably by his not caring about them today.

Billy was impressed. "Nice one! Hey – you want to come over and watch my Champions' League tape tonight?"

"Nah – not tonight. Kate's been on at me to do more reading."

About every four days, I see Dr Dunning. We all feel tired after we've been to the surgery. Kate mustn't drink the drink.

The little bus went by with the passengers staring straight ahead and went on past the man at the bus stop and out of town past the Danger of Death sign. Jake had to narrow his eyes to follow its progress. He was all at once aware how many reflective surfaces there were in this area of town. The pylon itself was shiny and caught the light. The Taylor's sign had a gloss finish, while the glasshouses were plain dazzling. No wonder it was a quiet place: people stayed indoors not only because of the heat but because if you stayed out here you were in danger of going blind.

Jake had a pound on him so he went back with Billy to the post office to spend some of it. Billy was occupied with his amazing ball skills on the way and Jake was able to look around without comment from his friend.

Because it still feels like he's my friend. It feels like he's a nice bloke, only with nasty eating habits. But what do I really know about Billy Smith?

The many windows on the top floors of the flour factory were more like mirrors than anything else, too. Three workers lounged around outside and one was smoking a cigarette. With his vision apparently keener over these last days, Jake saw how he didn't quite inhale, like he was an *amateur* smoker; and how when he dropped ash down the front of his overalls he brushed it away with some haste, nervously, as if the substance was strange to him and might be dangerous or set him alight or something.

They passed Mr and Mrs Barton's house, with Mrs Barton in the window, smiling like a dog, with uncontrollable lips. And knitting what exactly?

She doesn't know herself. The thought hit like a truth written in stone and though it was thirty degrees out here Jake felt abruptly cold.

Later the Higgins' played Monopoly. Very conscious of the hidden camera on the ceiling, Jake had to force himself to keep all his attention on the game. He was longing for the day to end because tonight he was going to venture out again to explore. The evening dragged and dragged. There was no fun at all in Monopoly when no one wanted to be a brutal capitalist and put others out of the game. For instance, lovely Kate offered to lend Stuart money when he landed on her hotels on Park Lane. Jake was sure he heard the light fitting above their heads do its clicking thing after Stuart said, "Don't be so foolish girl!" He went on, "That's no way to get on in life, is it?" and instead accepted Oona's offer of a loan. The light fitting didn't respond to that.

At last it was time for the drinks. Jake went to make them, relieved to be out of the front room. Thinking of the camera, he made himself a tea instead of chocolate because that way he could get a colour-match. He made sure Kate's drink was at least a little weaker than the others. In the living room he was careful not to sit too near any member of his family, who might pick out the smell of the tea.

At bedtime Oona said, "Oh you darling, come here! Ooh I do love you!"

"I love you too, Mum."

Smothered in her bosom, Jake was embarrassed at the idea that he was on camera. He hugged her, loving her all the same and feeling savagely protective towards her. He was going to do something about all this.

It took so long for everyone to go to sleep. Other than Jake, Kate was the last one to drop off, the well-worn thoughts that trailed across her mind becoming fainter and fainter. *I wonder what he'll be like… Won't it be terrible to leave Mum and Dad. New life is the most important thing there is. Who was that boy once? He was… He wasn't very nice…*

All was still. Jake could hear Kate's regular breathing, signifying sleep.

Now was the time. Be quick – be quiet. Out of bed; dress; down the stairs; no one in the front room tonight: good. Going too fast – bashed into the kitchen table. Halt and wait ... and it's OK and open the back door and out into the night, where the darkness was relieved by light from the Smiths' kitchen.

It had not rained again since that one time and the plants in the borders looked more forlorn than ever. His order of action was: first check on Billy, then ... explore. Method: using the brick wall at the bottom of the garden for reasons of noise and safer distance.

Very gently over his own wall, move low to Billy's. Hoist himself up to no more than eye level and hang on.

Billy was at his kitchen table with his mother, a plate of sandwiches and a man whose back was to Jake. The man had a dark tweed jacket draped over his chair and was hunched over a plate, eating.

Don't tell me it's going to be what I saw last night times three.

They were talking as they ate, Billy very cool and slow, while Mrs Smith appeared to have little input to make. The man ended the conversation with an impatient shake of his head and got up. As he turned to lift his jacket off the chair Jake saw that it was Dr Dunning who was the Smiths' visitor.

It was not a big surprise but it gave him a jolt all the same. If there had been any doubt in his mind before there was none now. Billy was not his friend and Dr Dunning was to be mistrusted too.

When was his next appointment with the doctor? Only a couple of days away – unless he were summoned to the surgery even sooner.

I've got to get on with this.

That was more easily thought than done. He was frightened and dreaded being seen. After several seconds' hesitation he decided to work his way up the waste ground to the back of the police station. He wanted to see where the road out of town led. Here the danger might come if he was spotted by someone in the flats. They were some way off, however, and only three lights showed in the array of buildings. As before, the urge for secrecy made him run in a crouching position along the hard earth. Well before he passed the hidden recreation strip, where the wall was a good five metres higher, another low wall loomed into view at right angles to the one he was hugging, cutting off his progress. From behind it an amber glow diffused the blackness. Maybe this obstruction was lucky for him, since because of it the police station could not overlook the wasteground except from its upper windows, which were dark. In a moment or two he should see past the pylon and the police station and see the direction the road took.

He was getting used to this. He jumped at the final wall and pulled himself up. It wasn't a long way to travel; but on the other side the drop was huge. The ground fell away sharply down to a big concrete basin below.

Jake sucked in a sharp breath as he took in just about everything at once. There was no road out of the town. Because it wound round the police station and curved down to end in this concrete car park. Beyond the pylon there was only the starry night sky.

The glow of light he had seen came from the police station windows on the ground floor. In the modest canteen were policemen and factory workers all jumbled up; sitting and talking together, or watching the TV, or playing pool, or eating. Then one of the policemen threw up into his hands and shoved the mess back into his mouth like a wadge of popcorn.

Even as the scene reached his eyes he was looking at something more shocking still.

Down in the bowl the local bus stood with its lights on inside; low in energy, they had enough strength to show that the passengers were all still on board, sitting passively in their seats just as they were when they motored by earlier in the day.

They never went anywhere. They turned the corner and eased down into a car park. One of Taylor's vans was there too.

Jake dropped back down on his side of the wall. He was breathing huge breaths to calm himself down.

This is worse than bad. What am I going to do? How does one get out of this place?

At least he felt comparatively safe here. No one came into the wasteland; it was just dead space between the houses and the flats.

That gave him an idea. Maybe it was different where the flats were. Maybe there would be a way through there. Maybe he was due some luck.

He began to trudge across the urban field in which no flowers grew. No flowers? No weeds, even. And it came to him that, surely, there should be bits and pieces of rubbish dumped here. But there wasn't even a crisp packet. Ah yes, but the inevitable wall was there. Quite low, though, this one.

Well, very low. In fact, progressively lower. In actuality only a metre high. Behind it, still some way off, the blocks of flats gave up their secret.

They were only twenty metres tall themselves.

They were giant models.

A light went off in one and farther down the rows of windows another came on immediately.

But Jake already knew there was no one home.

And he knew now there was no way out through the flats. Between the wall and the realistic models was a ragged chasm reaching far down into the ground; a natural fissure in rock.

And he had remembered what urban waste-ground should look like. He'd seen enough of it in his time. He'd run away from the orphanage. He'd lived rough.

How Stuart and Oona came into his life he couldn't remember at all. It was probably within the last five years because he'd had his tenth birthday in the orphanage. That had been one of the best days he had ever had.

Tonight was one of the worst.

5

It was bad. No way out and no one to tell because the first person they would consult was Uncle Jimmy; the brilliant fixer of all things for the Higgins family. Even Kate would think Jake had gone crazy.

Yes, but there *was* a way out. The way Uncle Jimmy himself took, down the hill, when he carried Stuart off on his motorbike to learn plumbing. So far Jake's researches had been confined to the area at the back of his house. The thought of it made him fearful, but he knew that now he had to venture out of the front door on his nocturnal travels.

Before he swept Stuart away today, Uncle Jimmy had a little news for them. He said, "Know what, you lovely people? I've put you in for 'Family of the

Week' – that thing Stevie Morrison does on the radio! How about that?"

"You mean," Kate said, " 'It's Awwl Right'?"

"That's him. Stevie Morrison. One of the good guys – Scots, like us."

"Like you and Mum," Jake corrected him.

"You're honorary, Jake – never forget it. He'll never find a happier family than this one, I can tell you!"

Yes … a "perfect" family nominated by a friend or well-wisher. Why did Jake feel so positive that it would be the Higgins who would be the winners this week? He'd never felt surer about anything. He caught Uncle Jimmy looking at him sardonically and couldn't help coming out with what was on his mind. "So – no one else stands a chance then – right?"

"Don't be silly, Jake," his mother said. "Oh, Jimmy, could you take in some dry cleaning for us? If it's on your way?" Which she knew it was.

He was glad to, and glad to hear that Jake was going to spend the day with Kate catching up on his reading: anything to do with the family and his learning difficulties was acceptable activity.

They had the house to themselves; it was Oona's turn to see the doctor. Jake wondered why he had never questioned their constant trips to the surgery, so handy just two doors away. Kate was going through one of his reading books with him, line by line. She'd thought they'd be in the front room or the kitchen, but he'd made her go up to their room, where they sat together on his bed. She'd remarked that he was acting oddly today and he thought *wait a bit and you'll think it's even odder*.

They'd been reading for a good half hour. Kate was nice; patient.

"So he says…?"

"It will be fun at the circus."

"Very good. And what does it say under the picture?"

That was harder. "Billy was so something he wanted to go … stag away."

"'Excited' and 'straight'. Can you see them now?"

"Sort of."

"So what does it say?"

Billy was so excited he threw up and ate it all over again.

"Billy was so … excited he wanted to go straight away."

"That's good, Jake."

It was really fine sitting so close to Kate, feeling her warmth and softness. Jake felt sad suddenly. Nothing lasted. Who knew what would happen over the next days. He thought back to the security of the house they had lived in before. No dwelling can compare to the first house you remember living in: that remains the HOME you think of as being ideal.

Except that in all likelihood there was something false about those memories too.

He said, "D'you remember the old house?"

"Of course." They had spoken of it before, allowing themselves the syrupy pleasures of nostalgia. "Mostly the living room. The fire ... that carpet with the flower patterns..."

Yes, the coal-effect gas fire that had flickered so warmly on winter evenings as they had sat on the old sagging sofa, with the long low glass-topped coffee table in front of them... The big mirror with candelabra-style double lights on either side...

"I wonder what happened to the sofa," Kate mused. "Well, it was very old. But we could have taken the coffee table with us. I sometimes think that when I've got a family I want a house just like that. Hey – are you trying to get out of doing any more work?"

"I'm kind of tired, Kate. Can we stop now?"

"Of course."

She had the book; shut it and put it to one side. They remained touching; close.

It had better be now. "Kate..."

"What?"

"It's..." This was much more difficult than he'd envisaged. "What I wanted to say was... Did you... Have you ever felt..."

"I don't know," she said wittily.

"There's something wrong here." It was said.

"Well, *you're* certainly acting very strange."

"All around us. Haven't you noticed anything?"

She dropped the banter. "Are you serious?"

"Our lives here – the place – it's all wrong."

"Don't be so stupid!" She flushed with anger and trotted out the old mantra, "We've got all we need – we've got each other – what more d'you want?"

It was a belief drummed into them and unshake-able. It had taken a lot for Jake to question it too.

Kate said, "I'm not going to talk to you if you're going to be so *stupid*."

So how did he tell her about all the throwing up and a bus–load of people who went nowhere because there was nowhere to go? He had to get somewhere with this though – at least touch first base. For now, one of the first clues, maybe. He said abruptly, "I can't walk past the pylon. Up the hill. Did you ever try that?"

"Now what are you on about?"

"Have you tried? Give it a go sometime."

"I could if I wanted to. You got any more nonsense to say or is that the lot?"

He was getting angry himself now. "Yes – and if it happens, remember I told you it would. We're the ones who are going to win that Family of the Week competition. Believe me, it's going to happen."

"You don't know any such thing. No one could."

"If we do, start *thinking*. And we'll talk. You can

always talk to me. But no one else. Not even Mum and Dad. They'd only tell Uncle Jimmy."

"And what's so wrong about that?" She was fidgeting with exasperation.

"It would be a mistake. Just believe me. You can only talk to me. You love me and I love you and there isn't anything more important in the world. OK?"

"I've had enough of this." She got up. So did Jake, and he held on to her arm.

"If something ever happened to me, would you promise me something?" He hurried on, "I want you to give up having the chocolate drink. As a favour to me. And not tell anyone."

"What?"

"And never tell anyone, even if you have to pretend you *are* having it."

"You're insane, you are. Nothing's going to happen – nothing ever does!"

He got passionate about it, gripping her too tightly. "I don't care. If you love me, promise, and *never* tell anyone."

She wrenched herself free, wanting an end to this whole nonsensical annoyance. "OK, OK, whatever. But I've gone right off you. You're being ridiculous."

"You promise?"

"I said, all right!" she said furiously. She got up and went downstairs, upset mostly because she didn't like thinking about anything happening to Jake.

Well, it was a start. He couldn't have said any more at this stage. She'd only blab it out to Stuart and Oona, too, laughing at him or teasing...

He went round to his part of the room. He'd have to work on her some more, though, if she was going to resist Dr Dunning's probing questions. Looking out of the window he saw the flats, standing so apparently tall; when you knew what they were really like you could see how you'd been fooled – you couldn't understand why you'd ever believed in them. They'd been *made* to see them as real, that was what it was.

All well and good to know they were fake. What lay behind them? Where exactly were he and his family living?

He felt obliged to spend time in the sitting room later. He had gone outside to catch Billy on his way to the Rec, to advise him that he was a bit beat and wouldn't be coming out today. Billy fixed him with those pale eyes. "Oh. Sure. What about tomorrow?"

"Oh yeah – sure – tomorrow, certainly. No question."

He watched the nature tape about the swans. Waiting. Being watched. Waiting. The day was interminable. In the evening the game was Racing Demon again. Jake lost badly, unable to concentrate.

Making the hot chocolate, he made sure Kate got an even weaker one than the night before. When she tasted it he could see she was about to complain, and then she shut her mouth and only gave him an exasperated look.

When he said goodnight to her, his "I love you," was exceptionally fervent. Just in case. She hugged him back strongly.

When her breathing had had last settled into the slow rhythm of slumber he slipped out of bed. He elected to put on his darkest clothes, which meant he had to wear the tracksuit top given to him by Billy in a moment of careless generosity, and began the night's work. He didn't go downstairs: instead he went into his parents' room at the front of the house, where their joint unconsciousness produced sporadic snores like small herd animals communicating to one another across the plains. He inched over to the windows and parted the curtains a fraction. There was always the possibility that the house was watched at night.

An hour later he was still at the window. While it did not seem that anyone was specifically detailed to watch the building, there was activity out there and some of it on a rota basis.

He'd never known. Badly lit by four sodium street lamps, the road was busier by night than by day. There was a constant, silent to-ing and fro-ing between the factory and the police station and the glasshouses of Taylor's Fresh Produce. Little groups of workers were out and about in their overalls, walking quietly and without conversation; sometimes they would be joined by other locals, who tended to come from Taylor's. What was very unsettling was the way that some of them walked, dragging their legs, or prone to uncoordinated jerks and freezes. This was something he had never noticed in the daytime. Then there were the policemen, walking in pairs but often joined by one or two civilians who were happy to keep them company. The officers of the law were on patrol and Jake was able to work out that they came by at half-hourly intervals. He was about to abandon his expedition when, shortly before midnight, the town settled down rather more. No doubt its citizens were at last taking to their beds. Nevertheless, the human traffic did not come to a complete stop and Jake would have abandoned his plan had he not laid such store by it. He had waited all day for this, after all. And if he was caught? What then? What could they do to him?

No. Perhaps it was better not to think about that.

He snaffled his father's keys from his jacket, and made for the stairs. Once down them, he needed a view of the road. He wedged the letter box open a tiny way. His field of vision was extremely limited, which made it hard to choose his moment.

It came after he saw two policemen go by unaccompanied. He reasoned that just to open the door and stick his head out couldn't land him in too much trouble and, setting the latch on the door so that he would be able to get back in, he counted to fifty and opened the door.

The warm night air welcomed him to a world in which he was the only visible living creature.

He had half an hour and if that wasn't enough he could come back, wait and go again. One way or another he would take a look-see at the way into town. He set off past the post office and had gone no more than five more paces before a figure appeared at the bend in the road. A factory worker, squat and wide. Jake froze.

The figure raised a hand.

"Hey," it called in a whisper.

Jake couldn't move.

"Hey … Billy!"

He couldn't think. He found he was raising his own hand in greeting and as it came up he too whispered, "Hey!"

He turned. Perhaps not tonight. Perhaps not *ever*. God, he was lucky. Mistaken for Billy – who always wore the same kind of top – that was an escape.

Only now he saw a group comprising three men and a woman coming at him from the direction of the recreation strip. Walking with that sinister caution, making no noise. He wanted to run into his house and lock the door behind him, but he knew that to do this would only delay some unpleasant outcome. Across the road, the dark portals of the flour factory stood open beyond the loading area. It was the only clear route open to him. Walk with purpose and just pray another bunch of them didn't come out from the factory.

He set off, keeping his head down. Halfway across the street he turned a little and raised his hand at the oncoming group. They all lifted their hands in greeting and – oh *no* – they were changing direction, crossing the road to follow him into the factory. He speeded up and went across the asphalt to where the wide open doors waited to swallow him.

There was no one around, no one waiting just inside to grab him. He went in. The factory entrance led straight into a large kind of lobby, in which countless white bags of flour were stored against the walls. The lighting here was recessed and, where it shone, orange – just enough to see by.

Just enough to spot that there were two people in here with him. A man and woman, pouring flour from one of the bags into a deep plastic bucket. The woman held the bucket while the man poured and it was she who saw Jake first.

"Hey, Billy… Nice!"

The man looked up, "Nice Billy!"

Billy's popularity was as much a threat to him as a defence. He couldn't go back, so once again he went on. "Hey," he said, the common greeting out here, hurrying past them on the other side of the lobby and working his way to the broad doors at the back, into which a smaller door had been built for human access. Inspiration struck – he picked up a bag of flour to shield his face with. The door within a door opened inwards. As he went through it he heard the party from the street arrive. "Billy," they said approvingly. "Billy," agreed the woman with the bucket.

He swung the door shut behind him. Safe for a moment. There was that crepuscular orange glow again and when his eyes had adjusted he saw that he had arrived in a space so large it would have been the main part of the factory. Only there was no machinery; no milling equipment. It was much more like a warehouse, with gigantic shelves set floor to ceiling all around the walls, divided by upright wooden supports so that they looked like a series of infinite bunk beds. Storage, but no machinery. Very, very strange. The lights here were positioned like "exit" signs above three doors; one at each side and one at the back.

Jake hesitated. This far in, he was going to have to take one of the doors. The one at the back? Truly, he was getting in deeper and deeper. He was never going to get to the road into town now. There was an alternative: he could climb the storage bays and hide near the top somewhere. He mustn't get driven any further in. He ran lightly to the left. Beneath the bays were piles of clothes – some of them factory overalls and some street-wear. All neatly folded in long rows, just lying on the flour-dusted floor.

Then behind him came the monotonous greeting from Billy's friends, who had come in after him, eager to get some response from the youth they liked so well.

"Hey, Billy."

"Billy."

"Billy."

Were his ears playing tricks now? There were more voices than there should be.

"Billy."

"It's Billy! Billy come!"

There were a lot more voices. He saw movement up and down the storage bays; there were stirrings as more and more of the sleepers awoke. If they looked like bunk-beds or berths it was because that was what they were. All around him.

A naked man was climbing down the supports from on high, from one of the top berths. There was something wrong with his arms and legs; they were black and withered as though burnt to charcoal. It didn't slow him down. On the contrary, he was one heck of a climber.

And so pleased to see Jake. "Hey, Billeeee!" he cooed as he came, his head screwed round to fix Jake with an affectionate gaze.

His happiness was infectious. Fifty voices joined in with the welcome.

"BILLEEEEE!"

"Hey, Billeee!"

Jake dropped his useless bag of flour. Someone queried optimistically, "Party? We have party tonight?" But he wasn't staying to talk about having fun with these people – he ran.

It was of course the far door he ran to. He felt rather than saw Billy's friends closing in from each side. He had no choice. Two steel doors opened automatically and a white light came on over his head.

"Not Billy!" came the exclamation. The light in here dimmed his vision of the vast dormitory but he could see vague shapes approaching.

"Who?" someone enquired mildly. Another voice was more threatening: "*Not Billy!*" With no great surprise he saw that on the steel floor at his feet there was a laundry basket and that protruding from it was a corner of Oona's smart red jacket, the one she wore when she visited Dr Dunning. The dry cleaning Jimmy was to have taken into town.

To his right there were some buttons in a panel by the doors. He pressed one at random and – oh glory – he'd got the right one: the doors slid shut. He could see his own reflection in the steel: a very frightened Jake.

Then the floor pressed against his feet and the room was travelling upwards.

He was in a lift.

It was a smooth ride, if a slow one. At last the
lift stopped and settled and the doors opened
automatically. Jake was in a state of shock and made
no attempt to hide; no preparation for instant flight.
It was in any case unnecessary. No one awaited him
here – wherever "here" was.

He didn't want to stay in the lift and didn't want
to leave it either. He could see it opened into a
modestly sized room built of old stone blocks. It was
round in shape and thickly carpeted, though
otherwise featureless except for an ancient-looking
stone stairway rising up off to his left and a curved
wooden door with iron studs in it. Action of some
sort became unavoidable when the lift doors began
to shut again. He darted forward, dragging the

laundry basket behind him, and positioned it to prevent the doors coming together. A couple of strides took him into the room, where his steps became soundless on the carpet. Should he take the door or the stairs? Would escape be more possible from the roof, perhaps?

He took the stairs. The stone treads were worn and dipped. The factory must be a lot older than he had thought. He went up the tight spiral, passing perpendicular window slits that were shuttered against the night. When he came to the next landing he was panting. The stairs were not illuminated in any way but here there was another heavy door and the faintest shaft of light came through the big keyhole in it. There were no sounds of pursuit coming from below so he took a moment to kneel and take a quick look through the keyhole. It led to some kind of long corridor – that much could be made out. He paused and listened. No sounds of pursuit came from below. Change of plan. What was he going to do on the roof? Hurl himself off? No – here was a clear run that could take him to a separate exit in quite another part of the building.

He tried the brass handle of the door and it turned easily. The door was heavy and, once he'd got it going, it swung open far wider than he'd intended. Still no one called out or rushed at him. After the masses gathered below to welcome their Billy, the silence here was unnerving. In the moonlight streaming in from a long line of tall, arched windows, he saw that the corridor could be more properly termed a room, one that stretched for metre upon metre, with a single narrow runner of a carpet running its length along deeply polished floorboards. He went straight to the nearest diamond-paned window and looked out and down. A confusion of soft hills descended down to a plain where, far off, something glinted. Not a house nor any other building to be seen anywhere. The land seemed to have remained untouched by man for centuries. Jake began to doubt that this terrain belonged in the industrial Midlands.

Turning from the window, he ran onwards. As he jogged along the strip of carpet he saw that on the facing wall the moonlight cast pale rays on high, mighty paintings of the high and mighty. Enclosed in gilded frames, men and women of other periods of history looked down on him disdainfully. A man in highly wrought armour, who had big eyes and a supercilious twist to his carmine mouth; women dressed as shepherdesses, and Victorian men of substance. There was also a series of curly-haired children presented as being so angelic that you felt they must surely have died tragically young.

In a flour factory?

Jake was jogging slower and slower, more and more bemused. Halfway down the long room he came upon a low door set into the wall on which the pictures hung. Its very lack of size suggested hidden secrets and at once he knew he had to see what lay beyond it.

The lever handle went down under the pressure of his hand and the door swung outwards a couple of inches – and something very pink rushed past.

He held his breath; heard running steps receding, and craned his head round the door to see. Someone in an almost fluorescent pink tracksuit was running a well-defined course, his back to Jake at this moment. The low door opened on to a gallery that swept all the way around the gigantic hall that lay below and it was round this minstrel's gallery that the figure was taking his exercise. A low, sinuous black creature darted along ahead of him. Was he chasing it? The man was about to turn now, at the end of the gallery where two proud mahogany stairways curved round and down towards each other on their way to the ground floor. Jake pulled the door to within a fraction of being wholly shut. He was disorientated. How high had the lift brought him up? This was surely no factory.

Wherever he was, it was definitely time to leave. That huge hall led to a front entrance, that was one thing he was certain of. The doubt was whether the pink running man was coming round again. Only one way to find out.

Jake opened the low door wide enough to see the length and breadth of the hall, with its arched ceiling, painted sky-blue and on which naked women were depicted lounging on a fluffy cloud which, considering the firmness of their ample flesh, could not have supported even the thought of them. But Jake would not have been interested had he been looking at one of the Seven Wonders of the World. There was no one around and he was out of here.

He sped lightly round the minstrel's gallery, following the path taken by the running man, arriving at the sweep of the first stairway and going down it two steps at a time. Halfway down, he stopped. Something was happening in the hall in front of him. There, at the other end of it, were the massive double doors he had hoped to see; and between him and that promise of freedom was an oak table reaching for metres along the centre of the hall and on each side of the table was a row of thirty high-backed chairs. The impression he got was of a kind of Round Table turned rectangular. Only … it was becoming two rectangular tables in front of his eyes.

The table was splitting down the middle, the two halves moving apart, and with them the chairs on each side. Jake took a few paces down the stairs. It wasn't the table that was splitting, he realized, it was the floor. It was dividing like the Red Sea; each section pulling back in a series of overlapping layers to reveal a dark sheet of glass.

When the chairs reached the walls the process

stopped. A wide lake of glass stood between Jake and the door. He came down the last steps and walked forward. Yellow patches of light could be seen through the dark glass, on to which he now put one tentative foot.

It was solid enough. Very solid, in fact. He began to walk its length and stopped. The patches of light came from street lamps way beneath his feet. He could see roofs and chimneys, and there, to his left, the glasshouses of Taylor's Fresh Produce.

He was standing on top of his own street, right above his own small house.

The opportunity to think was denied him when a bell began to ring up on the first floor: a handbell swung vigorously. At the same time lights came on all over the Great Hall, flickering into life one by one. He could still make it – he dashed for the main doors, slipping wildly on the glass, falling, careering in a slide to his target. A murmur of excited voices made itself heard and echoed in this great space and they seemed to be coming from almost every conceivable direction. The big rings that were the door handles turned all right but the door was locked. Any moment now the hall would be thronged with people. In the midst of his panic it came to Jake that if the rounded column over to his right had enclosed the lift and staircase then its twin on the other side of the mighty doors might offer an escape route. There was a door there, anyway – and he had reached it and had thrown it open just before he heard the voices reach the Great Hall.

Having closed the door so it was almost shut, Jake was in another of those almost circular rooms. It seemed that this place had towers on its corners – the front two, anyway. This chamber had a stairway but no lift. Well, maybe that was to the good. He ran up the twisting stairs, tripping where they were worn and uneven. His legs were shaking; not so much with physical effort as with nervous exhaustion.

So ... his home town comprised a single street built under the foundations of a much older structure. It made some kind of sense but at the same time only raised more questions. He tripped and stumbled up to the first floor and almost ran into danger. He heard slow, measured footsteps coming down from above...

OK. Through this open door here into what might or might not be another long picture room. Shut the door oh so gently. And let your eyes get used to the grey light from ... only four or five windows this time.

Feet pounded along the minstrel's gallery outside the room he was standing in. Here, instead of pictures, the inner wall was festooned with the heads of animals. A tiger, a buffalo, and many deer with horns of all sorts and all looking sad about their fate. Armchairs ... a writing table ... a leather sofa. It was some kind of living room, though who could want to live here with those mournful heads staring out was beyond him.

Then a voice came from outside the door he had entered through.

"Here, Sir – here! Come here at once, you dumb brute!"

Had he been seen? No. The voice would have summoned other voices, wouldn't it? Better get further away, all the same. Jake went on through the door at end of the room and closed it behind him as silently as he could. A bedroom, this was, with a giant four-poster bed and beautifully polished furniture from some old period; and there was … yet another door.

Jake had nearly had enough of this endless sequence of doors and discoveries, but it seemed wise not to try to hide in a bedroom when someone might be coming in to take their rest.

The next room was a dressing room. Tweedy clothes were strewn about everywhere. At the far end was a tall wing chair by an inlaid table and Jake sank down behind the chair to wait for whatever fate had to throw at him next.

He listened intently for sounds that might herald the arrival of the apartment's owner. In the insubstantial light from the windows he could see the corner of a Persian rug on those gleaming floorboards.

Now he heard it. A scratching, clicking sound as something approached from the direction of the bedroom he had come through. Something that snuffled unpleasantly and put its head round the back of the chair to gaze at Jake with dark eyes.

A dog. Black Labrador. It did not seem displeased to see him – he could hear its tail thumping against the arm of the chair. Its head went up and down, poking in at him to be stroked or welcomed or something.

He did not welcome it, nor the idea that its master was close behind it. While he still had the chance he got up and made his way to … the final door.

The dog followed, interested. Oh God.

He entered a bathroom, as was immediately obvious by the smell of soap and water and something faintly alcoholic. He shut the door to keep the dog out and leant his back on it. Too noisy to lock it.

Here was the master coming to his dog, *tramp tramp*, steady steps, and now the dog would whine and direct his master to the room in which Jake stood, tired and trembling.

The dog did indeed whine. Its owner said, in that whisky-muffled voice the man had, a sort of patrician slur, "Don't be silly, Trajan. Don't be so daft. Stupid dog."

And there was silence. *I bet he'll need to pee*, Jake thought despairingly, *or he'll want to do his teeth or get a glass of water…*

But apparently the man had no such needs. Jake came to understand that if you listened hard enough you could hear someone undressing and getting ready for bed. Only the man didn't go to bed. Instead a lamp came on. Maybe he had settled down to read, in that chair.

An age passed while the man did what he was doing and Jake did what he was doing – waiting without knowing what for. Trapped. As far as he could tell, there were no windows in this damp room. He felt a sneeze coming on and managed to suppress it.

Another age passed. An ice age – it was much colder up here than it had been in the place he'd come from, in the bowels of the earth. A place usually lit by what? Arc lights? Something like that, when it was "day".

Hello … movement in the room next door. Someone had come in. When the men talked he could hear them quite well and as clear as anything when he put his ear to the door.

The newcomer said something that sounded like, "Shonto."

The first man answered placidly, "Ortho."

"Problem," the visitor said crisply. The voice was teasingly familiar.

"Yes, old boy? What's that, then?"

"One of the subjects is on the loose."

"Oh dear."

"He may have got out already – but it doesn't seem likely."

"It doesn't?"

"I know it's too much to expect you to be concerned about this, Sholto, but it matters. To me."

Sholto. Strange name. Why did that other voice
sound as though he should recognise it?

"Ortho, if it matters to you, then it matters to me
– you know that."

"Just keep your eyes open, will you."

"Well, as you know, Ortho, my eyes are always at
your disposal."

There had been a definite edge to that remark and
it seemed to shunt the visitor on to another track.
"Yes ... how's your health? Keeping the exercises
up? Everything going well?"

"Orh, absolutely." Sholto's "oh" sounded much
more like "awe". Jake's mind registered that curiosity
at the same time that he processed another piece of
information. "*Everything going well?*" the visitor had
asked. On an instant, it came to him. It was the
routine question that Mr Roche, the relief postman
down below, was always asking. "*That's good*," he'd
said the other day, "*And everything going well?*"

It *was* Mr Roche. When he spoke again, Jake
was sure about it. That confident, cultured voice.
"Your annual outing soon. That's something to look
forward to."

"Orh, and I do, old chap."

"Let someone know, if you see anything."

"Of course."

Then, silence. The visitor had left, presumably. What to do now? Jake's dilemma was resolved for him. There was a double *click* right outside the bathroom door and Sholto's smothered voice said, close up, "You can come out now. Nice and quiet. Very very slow. I've got a Holland and Holland over-and-under pointing your way and if you do anything funny you'll get both barrels."

7

There were four holes boring into Jake as he came out of the bathroom. The over-and-under was a shotgun with the barrels set one on top of the other. As close as they were to his face, they seemed like the muzzles of cannons. Beyond and behind them were Sholto's eyes; piggy in the middle of swollen bags and yet of the brightest blue.

Standing there with his dog at his side, he was a man of about fifty-five with grey-blond hair that looked resinous and sticky. He wore a deep red paisley dressing gown and leather slippers and he had a lethal quality that had nothing to do with the gun he held; it came from a deadness within him that hinted at some missing component of intelligence.

Now he smiled, revealing small and perfect teeth

like those of a child. "Had you start to finish. Saw you when I was running. Led you here like beating a bird towards the guns! What d'you think of that?"

The man in the pink track suit. But he hadn't given him away. The thought made Jake calmer. "Did you shoot all those animals in the other room?" he asked.

Sholto backed slowly, keeping the gun trained on Jake. "Every one of them. Grand sport. I have twenty-twenty vision and a very steady hand."

"I'm not going to try to run."

"That's wise."

"Who were you talking to?"

Sholto jerked the shotgun and Jake winced. "Get into the drawing room."

When they had accomplished this journey by a sequence of dance-like, co-ordinated moves that were continually impeded by Trajan's need to get himself underfoot, Sholto indicated for Jake to sit on a chair he placed in the middle of the room. After turning on a couple of lights the hunter then went to his writing desk and set down the shotgun, only to take an automatic pistol from a drawer. He loaded the gun with speed born of long practice. Keeping it by his hand, he broke open the shotgun and removed the cartridges. Then he picked the pistol up again and held it to his nose to smell it. "Mmm. Gun oil. Nothing like it. It's a Browning," he explained. "Very basic handgun; can jam on you. Wouldn't risk it, if I were you, though."

"What do you want," Jake asked bluntly.

"I'm a man of my word," Sholto answered obliquely in that muffled voice. "Trust me, young man, it's a burden. Now you, you started out dishonest and, believe me, your path in life will be much easier because of it."

"What do you know about me?"

"Absolutely nothing. A piece of human flotsam gathered up by my heroic older brother."

"The man you were talking to?"

"The man I was talking to. Ortho. Not what he was christened, of course. A very, very great man. Orh yes, no doubt about that. You could see that from the start. He saved my life, you know, when we were boys. Dragged me out of St Agnes' loch when I fell out of the boat. Only four – couldn't swim yet, d'you see."

"The loch?" said Jake. "Where are we then?"

Sholto looked irritated at being interrupted. "Scotland. And the old brother gave me his blood, when I had a hunting accident. Rare group, you understand. 'All I ask,' he says, 'is that one day you repay the compliment.' Then his ghastly mob took the idea up – came to me with a suggestion – and Ortho went along with it. They're an appalling crew, always have been."

"Who are?"

"SCOM."

"Scom?"

Sholto was again annoyed by Jake's obtuseness. "Society for the Continuance of Mankind. His acolytes. Put it to me that here was not only a great scientist, but a great man. One so great that he mustn't be allowed to die if there was any way of preventing it. I couldn't see any way out, so I agreed. Agreed that if ever there was the need, my body parts would be his. It seemed only right, in the circumstances. What with him trying to save the world and me doing nothing you could remotely call useful with my life. Well, they were doing heart transplants then; but no one had the courtesy to explain to me that soon they'd be able to patch in spleens, livers and lungs as well. I've never made a secret of my superb eyesight, and you should have seen their unbounded delight when *that* operation became theoretically possible. 'Just keep yourself fit,' they said. Laid down a strict regime. But I did get lovely things – guns and stuff – things I needed. Only a kidney's worth, if you ask me, all told. Not a fair exchange for every organ in the human body."

"I'm not getting any of this," Jake said.

"Good God, you're a fool. Thought I was the stupidest man on earth till you came along. I'm telling you, I gave my brother a kidney two years ago. He drives himself too hard. No knowing what's going to go next. I said to them, 'Here's one of the greatest scientists who ever lived – couldn't you ask him to try his hand at cloning? That's the way,' I said, 'You get a perfect replica of your beloved Ortho and you can just cut bits off as the need arises.' They said it was contrary to their beliefs. They would say that – typical Hippie nonsense. Terrific idea, cloning – absolutely marvellous. Clone yourself a healthy body and keep it on ice for when it's needed. In America these rich industrialists have piles of them lying around, I shouldn't wonder. Ortho never listens to me, of course. The older brother, d'you see, head of the family – real name, Sir William Carrick-Boyd. You'd think with all the responsibilities he has he'd feel obliged to take care of himself. But he won't. Should take a leaf out of my book. I wrote out a simple exercise programme for him to follow, but did he do it? Did he, bottom."

Sholto brooded on his grievances. Seated by his side, Trajan looked up at him with deferential adoration.

His master spoke again with vehement bitterness. "Thing is, I gave my word. If you call yourself a gentleman, you keep your word. What other value have I got? But them – are they gentlemen? Not a bit of it. The frailer he gets, the less freedom I have. Allowed to go out shooting just once a year! Can't leave the building! Can you believe that? So you can see that when I saw you I began to see some light in the situation."

He had spent only a few minutes in Sholto's company, but Jake was fed up with him already. "I can't see anything at all. What is this 'SCOM' business? Why are we living in that world down there?"

All at once, Sholto looked cunning. "Aha. Orh. Well … I can't tell you. It's a matter of 'need to know', d'you see. If I was to tell you certain things you might go telling someone else and I could get into a lot of trouble. This way, I'm an innocent party, ignorant and everything and only concerned 'cos someone has been held against his will. D'you get it – how clever I'm being? Get it?"

"I was kidnapped – is that what you're saying?"

Sholto laughed out loud. "I don't know! That's the whole point!"

"But you're going to help me? Am I right about that?"

"I'm going to get you out of here. I can't leave but you can. Solves everything. Then you do whatever you have to and Bob's your uncle. Just remember this: *I know nothing* and if you say any different I'll find you, shoot you, cut your head off, and stick it up with the others."

"What do you think I ought to do when I get out? You think I should—"

He was shushed very quickly. "No – no – don't tell me. I'm just a bumbling fool who's helping you out."

"All right – all right. Just tell me what this place is."

Sholto considered, contemplating out loud whether an answer to this would incriminate him. "I don't think you'd know exactly where you'd been taken … but on the other hand, you meet this friendly, innocent chap and he's got no reason not to tell you… 'My God, I can hear you saying, old Sholto Carrick-Boyd deserves a medal.' Yes. Right – we're in Broomcleuch Castle, in the Border Country. Somewhere sort of between England and Scotland."

"I thought we were in the Midlands," Jake said faintly.

"Orh no. The Border Country. The second most uninhabited area in Scotland, let alone England. Let's think … what else would I have told you? Nothing. Nice, but not too bright – that's me."

And he fell silent. They sat there.

Sholto looked at his watch and pulled a grumpy face in a way that said the hands weren't moving fast enough.

Jake said, "So, let me go, then."

Sholto was cross with him. "No, no, no. You don't understand at all. You've got to have something to say that'll bring people here. *I* can't tell you anything. I'm a man of my word. You have to hear it for yourself. We have to wait."

"But—"

"Shut up, you little turd, or you can dig a bullet out of your brain right now."

Jake shut up. Already the fragments of knowledge he had were lacerating his brain as one of Sholto's bullets might have. A fake town. Under a castle in Scotland. Some kind of secret society run by a man he had believed was a relief postman, whose name was Carrick-Boyd. And he, Jake, had been kidnapped? Where from? He guessed it had been from nowhere special. He had lived on the streets. Human flotsam. The word conjured up a small piece of rubbish lost and floating on dangerous ocean. Apt enough.

After repeated reference to his watch Sholto said at last, "That should do it. On your feet."

"We're going now?"

"We're going *somewhere*," he was answered cunningly. "You first. Don't make a sound – don't make a move – don't do anything. You've only got to hiccup and I'll shoot you. Got it?"

"Yes. Seems clear enough."

"Shut up," Sholto said testily. "And get moving."

He stuck the gun in Jake's back and they went out of the apartment. Trajan was left inside and started whining. Sholto hissed testily, "Oh shut *up*," through the door. They were going to do something that made the man nervous and that was all Jake got from his petulant behaviour.

Down in the Great Hall someone started speaking and when they got near the gallery Sholto made Jake crawl the rest of the way on his belly; a command he issued via a dumb charade that involved a lot of gun-waving.

It was that voice again. The one he thought he knew. Ortho. Worming his way to the gallery railings, Jake heard the words resonating as if it were an address by a bishop in a cathedral.

"You are downcast. We are all of us shocked. I ask you, in this moment of doubt, to meditate for a moment. Recall the purity of our purpose. Remind yourselves how the future of the human race is in our hands. Reflect how we are guided from Above. Listen to the hope in your hearts and not to the fear in your minds."

Behind Jake, Sholto whispered, "Take a look and keep your head down!"

Jake reached the point where he could peer down through the wooden railings. The long table was back in one piece and all around it sat men and women in various states of undress, summoned as they had been from their beds. Ah. He had been right. The mystery voice did belong to Mr Roche, of all people... He was on his feet at the top end of the table, head bowed in spiritual contemplation. Only, of course, he was really Sir William Carrick-Boyd, a.k.a. "Ortho", a compact figure in a check shirt and dark corduroy trousers.

Looking around, Jake saw there was a contrast between the grandeur of the setting and the men and women that were now gathered here, who could have been mistaken for Travellers in their jeans and hand-made clothing. Some still wore their dressing gowns; all had faces lined with age and, though their hair was long, it was grey or even white in some cases. And one of them was Billy Smith's mother, dressed in a loose cotton caftan, sitting at the bottom of the table in the place one might find the hostess of the party.

Now Ortho, as Jake would henceforward think of him, murmured in prayer, "Lord, we bring to mind the many innocents doomed to suffer for the foul achievements of the few and our strength is renewed."

He raised his voice again. "Our journey has been a long one and strewn with errors made in good faith. We have never despaired. Remember when we were young – the earnest discussions we had about the evils of nuclear warfare. Remember the cameraderie of the Aldermaston marches! Our passion to save the world! In our work we went too fast. For that I am to blame. We created children who by their hybrid nature were unable to live in society. But we love them and have never abandoned them. They are our children, our beloved brood. And is *their* sacrifice to be in vain now? Now we know the optimum breeding age? Now we have the technique refined and at our disposal? Now we are so close, with the prospect of sending out our first carrier in only a few short weeks? Kate. Kate

Higgins. The first free-roaming breeder of an improved human race. Her name will live in the annals of history." He grew louder and more strident. "We must not fail her; we must not fail ourselves; we *cannot* fail the generations yet unborn!"

It had an effect. His listeners sprang to their feet and applauded. With the noise of it ringing in his ears Jake gulped inwardly.

They were doing something to Kate and, he gathered, it involved a process that had gone wrong in the past. A carrier? *A breeder?* The phrases made him shudder.

Mrs Smith still had that resigned, hopeless way about her as she got to her feet and called down the table to Sir William.

"I feel I should go back down below, Ortho. The children will be worried and my place is with them."

"No need, Lavinia," he answered her crisply. "The children are happy. They can manage quite well without you."

One of the elderly Travellers rose now with a request. He was a big man with iron-grey hair cut comparatively short and he had a wispy Highland accent. "The bulletin, please, Ortho. I must return to Team Two."

"Very well," Ortho answered. "Mr Seton-Lindsay is on his way, but I can begin to brief you all in his absence. The fundamental point to hold on to is that nothing has altered. The team member who has absconded was the least necessary to the group: his role was merely to provide added protection for the Carrier. His knowledge is non-existent; his memory is missing: in short, should he be questioned his sanity would soon be a matter of serious doubt."

"And were he to be returned to SCOM?"

"He is unstable and has no more use to us."

"I mean, Ortho, what action would be taken?"

Ortho pondered for a moment, leaning forward to hold the edge of the table. Then he straightened up once more. "When mistakes have been made in the past, we have been painfully aware that involuntary sacrifice is a price that must be paid in pursuit of a great cause. This is a boy who now has no history and never had a future."

"I'm sorry, Ortho," Lavinia, mother of Billy Smith, put in, "But we have never countenanced the taking of life."

Another voice entered both the debate and the hall itself. Dr Dunning, in his suit, had arrived from the tower that held the lift. He was dispassionate as he approached the table.

"His life would remain intact. His brain would be the object of our attention. The boy could be reduced to a level at which he could live amongst the children."

"Ralph," Ortho said warmly, "the floor is yours."

Dr Dunning took up his station at Ortho's side.

Standing under the high, painted ceiling he looked entirely at ease in the grand surroundings.

"The necessity for surgery is here," he said. "He opened up the sky last night. Which control he used we don't know, but how he fathomed its use at all must give us pause. At the very least, he knows more than he should."

And I'm learning more by the minute, Jake thought. He shot a look over his shoulder at Sholto, who crouched behind him with the gun. The twenty-twenty eyes looked back at him very shiftily.

Mrs Smith – if that really was her name – queried, "Surgery?" in tremulous tones.

Dr Dunning dismissed her doubts out of hand. "A very minor operation. Or one might employ invasive chemical agents. It's a fine detail just now."

But he wasn't known as Dr Dunning here. Ortho said, "Mr Seton–Lindsay has good news for us, I understand. His projection is that the team may well benefit from this experience."

"Indeed," said Seton–Lindsay. It was extraordinarily easy to dislike him once you removed the "Doctor" from his name, Jake found. "I saw at once how this event, which will doubtless initially be perceived by the team as a tragedy, might in actuality be the thing that pulls these individuals together in a way that no artificial means can accomplish. It may be, in fact, the final bonding agent. Not, you understand, that there is any question of ceasing to apply the techniques of chemical psychology – far from it – but where possible organic processes must be allowed to take place. Only a week ago this might have undone all our work, but now I foresee little chance of deterioration amongst the remaining trio. There may be some signs of regression, true, but overall the prognosis is remarkably good."

Another man spoke and once more Jake thought he recognized the voice. Deep and at the same time quick, it was Scottish and sounded remarkably like that of Stevie Morrison, the radio disc jockey.

"Mr Seton-Lindsay, with the skills you have at your disposal, could not the boy be returned to his family – I mean, the team – were he to be found?"

"It would be an unacceptable risk to reunite him with the team, mission-critical as it is. He has broken free once already. I ascribe this in part to his dyslexia. So many of our reinforcements are word-based. Even the subliminal images inserted in the videos are often captioned. In our sessions together I have found him to be a recalcitrant individual and, quite frankly, the ideal solution would be complete termination."

The big Highlander rose to his feet and said in his gentle tones, "Well, Mr Seton-Lindsay, you will be following our path or we'll no more deal with you. He that speaks of termination may bring it on his own head. I'd be reminding you of that."

Ortho intervened. "Please, please – enough. We

do not expect Mr Seton-Lindsay to embrace our beliefs. For his part, I know he is wholly committed to our work and that is all that concerns us."

"That is so," the doctor-who-wasn't concurred blandly. "And now if you'll excuse me, I must get on with things. It's unfortunate timing, but pharmacy stocks are low and only I can replenish them, as you know. Since we're all up and about I'll start out right away, in order to return the sooner. The team will remain under observation and the simpler drugs will be administered as necessary."

"Fine, Ralph. Off you go," Ortho said. It was hard to tell how friendly the two men were, but clearly they had a good working relationship. "And for the rest of us, those designated will relieve the search party while the others take up stations within the castle."

A general buzz of conversation was starting up even before he finished. "This situation is manageable, ladies and gentlemen."

Jake felt a tugging at his ankle. As the party downstairs broke up he too was due elsewhere. He was made to crawl ahead of Sholto, back to the apartment. Once safe behind closed doors he bombarded Sholto with questions which the man would not answer. He was in a state about something.

Jake said, "Just tell me why I was brought here – just tell me what it's about. What's a Carrier? What's going to happen to my sister?"

"You've heard too much already," Sholto retorted angrily. "I'd no idea they'd say all that."

When Jake persisted he raised the muzzle of the Browning with blinding speed and pointed it directly at Jake's head. His eyes shone. "The one thing I've not yet shot is a man. Dreamed about it, naturally."

"You wouldn't shoot me," Jake bluffed. "You want me to get out of here."

"Not so sure now. Trying to think it over."

"And what was that about me opening up the floor? I never did anything."

"Ah, well, perhaps not."

"It was you." Jake blurted out the thought as it arrived.

"Well, I was pretty quick," Sholto said modestly. "Orh yes. Thought on my feet and the whole thing came to me. Did it a few nights before too – just to try and stir things up. The idea was, 'Someone sees something, someone gets out'. But now, well, I don't know. Can't get a picture of it any more, somehow, in my mind. Seems to me you know too much now."

He was glowering at him with deep suspicion so Jake tried some reassurance. "I wouldn't do anything that'd make trouble for you."

For some reason he'd said exactly the wrong thing and Sholto's voice became even more muffled through explosive emotion. "There you are, you see! It's on your mind – betraying me – you brought it up! *You* – not me. Like the chap who farts at school and asks who did it – you know it's him!"

"But I wouldn't betray you. I bet your first idea was the best."

"You don't think it's a little risky? I do! When here we are standing here like this and it could all be so neat. One shot and I'm a hero, according to Ralph Seton-Lindsay. They might even let me choose my own food."

Sholto advanced the gun until it came to rest against one of Jake's eyes. "'He attacked me,' I say, 'Came out of nowhere.' Then *they* say, 'My golly, Sholto, you're one hell of a chap.' Good scenario. *Very* good scenario. Clean and simple."

He meant it. Because, as Jake was beginning to understand, he was kept sequestered here not just as body-parts for the brilliant brother, but because he was quite definitely mad.

"It'd be wonderful, to shoot someone," Sholto said with wet anticipation. "See them drop…"

Trajan started to whimper.

With the one eye that that was open, Jake could see Sholto's finger tightening on the trigger.

8

In the instant of life left to him, Jake saw that Sholto's eyes were glazed; the gun-obsessed aristocrat was lost in the overwhelming thrill of the moment.

The knuckle on his trigger finger was whitening.

Jake said, "Too easy. Not much sport." It came out as a croak.

"I beg your pardon?" The bright blue eyes became more focussed.

"This is how you shot everything else? Right up close while they were standing still? Doesn't exactly take twenty-twenty vision, does it? My grandmother could do it."

If I've got a grandmother, of course. The absurdity of thinking such a thought at such a time made him smile despite himself and the remnants of Sholto's deadly purpose were blown away on seeing the grin.

He lowered the gun a fraction and said in quite a friendly, confidential way, "Hang on... Are you saying I should give you some kind of a start, and then – what – track you down with a rifle – is that the idea? Not really practical, you know."

"Yeah ... I know. Um, maybe we'd just better forget the whole thing."

"Mmm. Perhaps you're right," Sholto agreed. He frowned. "So – I'm sorry – where does that leave us?"

"Plan A? You get me out of here? When it's safe? I can't really see anything against that one. I'd have thought it'd be good to find someone you can count on. I mean, I've been lonely myself now and then. It's not easy, I know, making all your decisions for yourself."

A trace of moisture came to Sholto's brilliant eyes. "Well, no, it isn't. You do have a point. There's more to you than at first appears. Orh yes. Now then. Get you something to eat. Don't want you to starve to death, do we?"

Keeping an eye on Jake, he opened a cupboard door to reveal a small refrigerator.

While it was a relief that they were back on friendly terms, Jake knew that his host's pathological volatility could still be a problem and he resolved not to upset Sholto in any way again. He would ask no more awkward questions and would pretend compliance in everything. All with the sole aim of getting out of here.

Outside, he had a chance of saving Kate from whatever fate awaited her. In here, he had none. If he was sure of anything it was that Kate's interests would be at the forefront of his thinking. She was trapped down there amongst those – what could he call them? Dormitory dwellers? The townspeople below. He wondered how he could ever have believed them to be normal, everyday human beings. He suspected strongly, now, that Kate was not his sister, but she was still herself, warm and loving, and she needed his help more than she could ever imagine.

When at last laid out on the table, the meal was insubstantial. It appeared that in the interests of his health Sholto was restricted to grains and pulses and skimmed milk and a variety of juices.

"If you want some meat I haven't got any," he said heavily. "Not allowed. But Trajan's got some tins, if you're desperate."

Jake wasn't.

"Ghastly muck," Sholto said, tucking into a bowl of health-giving muesli. Afterwards he had a low fat spread on a diet biscuit and a cup of camomile tea, at which he pulled a face like a child drinking medicine.

"Coffee," he said, "that's the stuff for a man. And a little gin at lunchtime, whisky and wine at the end of the day. Can't remember when I last had a drop of port. No stimulants, they say. Generations of Carrick-Boyds lived long and well on nothing but stimulants. What's the world coming to. Should be thankful we've still got the ancestral home. The new one, that is. Only built at the end of the eighteenth century, but I love it. Always been my home. Don't know what I'd do if anything happened to it. Frenchy sort of architecture. When you see it you'll see what I mean. Much like a corner of Holyrood House – you know the kind of thing."

Apparently starved as much of company as rich victuals, Sholto was a talker – but he wouldn't talk about the things Jake wanted him to. Now he said, "Built on the ruins of a medieval Abbey. They had these deep, deep foundations – cellarage and so on – hence when they came to plan the…"

He trailed off and shot a glance at Jake, who said innocently, "It must have taken some work to create … all that down there."

Sholto ruminated on how to respond to this. "Don't know what you're talking about," he said triumphantly, at last. They then fell into a companionable kind of silence until the moment Sholto clutched at his chest, rose in a panic without forgetting to take his pistol with him, and scurried to his desk to open the only book in the whole apartment. It was a medical dictionary of some substance.

He flicked through the pages and found the place he wanted. "'Myocardial infarction,'" he panicked aloud. "Or maybe 'pulmonary stenosis' – or what about 'aortic incompetence'"?

He looked over wildly at Jake, who had a polystyrene-type biscuit suspended halfway between plate and mouth. "Or gas. Tell me it's gas."

"It's gas?" Jake suggested, hoping to please.

Sholto calmed down. "Gas – yes. Simple heart-burn." He glowered across at his empty cereal bowl. "Small wonder, when they feed you like a *duck*."

He came back to the table, bringing the book with him for further studies. Even while he perused it he kept his gun in a state of readiness to shoot his guest. Small sounds of horror escaped from him and then whole sentences. "Beastly reading. Beastly. Should never open this damn book. Should never have taken an interest in the first place. You have no conception of how many ailments there are out there waiting for you. Or for your brother… Just think, he could have 'Tetralogy of Fallot' and no one's spotted it. Yet. Where would I be then?"

He closed the reference book with reluctance. "Undergoing removal of the old blood pump, that's where." He gazed at the windows disconsolately and then looked unlovingly at Jake. "Greedy little beggar, aren't you. You want to watch it or it's a peptic ulcer for you. Can lead to a total gastrectomy, I seem to recall."

"When do we go?"

"Got to let the chase die down. The hunted animal goes to ground if he can. Orh – and a word of advice. Be careful who you talk to when you do get out. The Laird of Broomcleuch is a man of influence in these parts and half the countryside thinks he's God. Spies everywhere, I shouldn't wonder."

They waited. And waited. He was so tired and he knew he couldn't sleep though every nerve in his body begged him too. Some time later Jake's head came up off the table with a jerk. Someone was shaking his shoulder.

"Don't know how you can snooze at a time like this," Sholto complained in his indistinct voice.

"Time like what?" Jake mumbled, bewildered because he was somewhere other than the place he had thought of as home.

"Time to go."

And it all came back in a rush.

Sholto was in his pink tracksuit, dressed for action. "God, you're an an untrustworthy-looking little brute," he said, beginning to worry all over again.

"No – really – you can trust me. I won't say anything." Jake wasn't going to let the chance go now, not after all he had been through.

When they left the apartment Trajan was over-joyed to discover he was included in the party. "My alibi," Sholto said affectionately, patting the dog's head. He opened the door to the landing and for the first time Jake let himself believe that in a few minutes he would actually be free.

Sholto took them down the winding tower steps to a level beneath the Great Hall, an area lit by naked light bulbs hanging from the vaulted ceilings.

"Utter silence. Kitchens. Nearly morning," he whispered, holding the ever-present Browning to his lips. There was no electric lift on this side of the castle, but out of the corner of his eye Jake caught sight of the start of a metal spiral staircase leading down somewhere to the world below.

They went along a stone-flagged corridor past an archway and into the kitchens, though only after Sholto had peeped in to see if anyone was present. But it seemed that no one was about. At the end of the corridor was a sturdy door built for men of short stature.

"No locks here you see. But bloomin' rowdy bolts," Sholto said in a low voice. He was right. There were four bolts, and the scraping sound of iron on iron seemed deafening as he worked them. The door opened ponderously on to a small court-yard, ghostly in the moonlight. "I have the use of this door for when Trajan needs to do his business, you see. Couldn't be better. Now then. Got it straight in your head what you're up to?"

"Think so. I'm going to—"

Sholto danced about in an ecstasy of irritation. "Don't tell me! I'm a man of honour! I don't want to know! When you see someone all *you* know is that a nice man helped you when you were wandering about but he was a kind of prisoner and the rest you discovered for yourself. Which you did. Are you with me?"

"No. What's the matter with the people down there – where I came from?"

"What people?" Sholto said evasively. "Listen. If you come back here I'll shoot you on the spot. And watch out for the guards as you go – they're armed."

"Ah. Thanks," Jake commented wryly. "But you've got to tell me – what exactly is it that's wrong with everyone down there?"

"You're driving me mad! Go on – get out. Get out." Sholto had to grip on to Trajan's collar for all he was worth as the dog very actively anticipated an excursion outside. Jake saw how flustered Sholto was getting and persisted. "Go on – just tell me. Who are all those people down there?"

Alarm, or horror, clouded the blue eyes. Horror because Jake just wouldn't leave?

Sholto said, "They're not people."

He pushed Jake out into the night and shut the door on him.

* * *

Getting past the SCOM guards was quite easy. Over the years they had relaxed in the application of their duties and after the passage of several hours had little thought of finding the runaway so close to home. The first moments had been the worst, when he had gone up the short flight of steps leading out of the courtyard to spy out the land.

The terrain was as he'd seen it from the picture gallery. Broad, serene and hilly, its softness was explained by the length of the grass. The land dropped away from all sides of the castle that loomed over him, and was much more uneven than it had appeared from his previous vantage point, being ridged and hollowed where scars of the past had healed and settled over the centuries. Low trees had been deformed by the winds that had free play over the uplands; and the guards, when he saw them, very helpfully shone torches to advertise their presence, carried in order to negotiate the bumps and dips without accident.

He'd watched two such men go by at some distance before he felt brave enough to set off from the castle. A tarmac road wound up to the main doors of the building and he kept well away from it, stumbling through the knee-length, night-dewed grasses, going from tree to tree and moving ever faster as the deep loneliness of the night worked its spell on him. Wherever he ended up, it had better be somewhere warm. It was an exceptionally cold autumn out here for one used to endless discussions on how uncomfortably sunny the weather was.

When he had been travelling for fifteen minutes he turned to look back. Broomcleuch Castle stood on its remote eminence, tall and elegant in its simplicity. The curves of the towers on all four corners relieved any hint of austerity and behind the crenellated walkways, the conical roofs of the towers lent the castle a foreign and legendary aspect. Had it been daylight he might have admired its most unwar-like beauty; but outlined against the night sky it suggested a place of sorcery and torture.

And Kate was still in there. Or under there.

He needed to get to a phone.

Yes. Now he had a purpose. And this was the safest way. Only trouble was, it didn't exactly look like the kind of area where public telephone boxes proliferated…

His train of thought was interrupted by a high snarling sound. A mechanical noise – a motorbike.

Uncle Jimmy's?

He's not my uncle.

Jake raced downhill faster still, seeking out the next stunted tree on his course. He tripped and rolled the last metres through the grass, so that he was soaked from head to toe now, rather than below the knees only. But he made cover in time to escape detection when the motorcycle made its appearance atop one of the ridges above. The engine deepened as it slowed and, keeping himself pressed into the rough bark of the tree trunk, he had the uncomfortable idea that he'd been spotted earlier.

The rider was not Uncle Jimmy. He or she was a slight figure in black, riding a sleek bike which looked like one of those designed to go cross-country, only with two panniers at the back. Probably one of the guards – a SCOM member detailed to patrol the outer limits of Ortho's territory.

Maybe he hadn't been seen, though. The bike now accelerated away from his hiding place, topped a small rise and disappeared, the engine sounds immediately becoming much fainter. Jake waited, aware that this might be a ruse of the rider to flush him out, but when he had not heard the motorcycle at all for several minutes, he went onwards.

Way off to his right he saw the squat shape of an old square tower. It overlooked a copse of trees as though set there to make sure they did not wander off, an antiquated warrior retired from service for hundreds of years. Beyond the trees was a sheen of light. Jake changed direction to head for the grim little tower and changed direction again when he heard the motorcycle returning. This time he had the bright idea of throwing himself face down in the grass, hoping that the night rider would not come close enough to spy him.

Again the bike's engine faded. Jake got to his feet, shivering violently. The moon shone full for a moment, breaking free from clouds, and the sheen of light was everywhere in front of him and to both sides. He was near the edge of a great stretch of water. And there was a thin little rowing boat pulled up on its bank.

The bike was coming back. Jake ran for the old rotting boat and climbed in as into a coffin. It fitted him all too snugly. When the bike moved on again – did it never need petrol? – the idea came to him. If he had to go round the margins of this massive lake or whatever it was, he was constantly in danger of discovery, from the bike rider or someone else. Whereas, if he took to the water, he might just get … wherever he was going somewhat quicker. Certainly more safely.

Or so he thought.

There were no oars in the boat. He discovered, however, that forward motion was possible if he lay face forward in the bows and used his hands to push the water away on either side of the prow. It was wondrously peaceful, paddling steadily through the freezing water in the silver light and he was almost beginning to enjoy himself when two factors became apparent. There, across the water were pin-pricks of light twinkling from what must be a pretty substantial building, so it could be said that taking to the water had been a good choice; but at the same time there came the creeping certainty that the freezing water outside the boat had not confined itself to its natural bounds – it was making its way up through the bottom of the old boat at an alarming rate. Jake jiggled about by way of research and icy wetness sloshed over his back.

The boat was sinking, fast.

Well now. With none but recent memories available to him, he had no idea whether or not he could swim.

At night he dreamed sometimes that he could swim.

He dreamed too that he could fly.

Dawn was about to break. As it filled, the rotting hull in which he lay settled deeper into the water and forward motion ceased.

Kate was not used to being anxious like this. It hurt, so disturbingly that she did not at first recall the argumentative conversation she'd had with Jake.

"He'll be up at the Rec. Lovely morning like this," Oona said. Her face was crumpled with worry, however.

Stuart and Kate went out. The sun had only just come up but the light was as dazzling as ever. Jake was not at the Rec.

One of Taylor's greenhouse staff was up already too, washing the brilliant windows of the glasshouses. "*Lovely* day," he assured them, with a strangely frightened sidelong glance.

Passing him, Kate caught a sweet rotting smell in

the air around the fresh produce retailers. She had a keen sense of smell and every now and then you got that odour in the air and it rather put you off the idea of buying anything at Taylor's.

Mr Barton was leaving his house to insert himself into his three-wheeler. Mrs Barton hovered near him to say goodbye.

She said it. "Goodbye." It was all she said.

"Goodbye," he answered dully. And got into his car. They didn't hug, didn't touch at all. Kate thought, *They're not loving, like we are. The thing about love is how painful it is when things go wrong.*

When they knocked, Mrs Smith came to the door of the post office in her dressing gown. She knew nothing about Jake.

"It'll be all right. Nothing could happen to him, not here. He'll be *fine*," she reassured them. Her very animation was all wrong, so unlike her. Billy came up behind her and they questioned him too. He stared at Kate all the time, the way he always did, and she did not much care for it.

"Oh, he'll turn up somewhere. I'll look out for him. You look nice, Kate."

He really did have to like her a lot to say that; she'd dressed and brushed her hair very quickly and without care when it had become apparent that Jake was nowhere around the house.

When Uncle Jimmy came the Higgins were frantically pleased to see him. As they babbled and gabbled about where on earth Jake could be they forgot all about having the morning drink and it was Uncle Jimmy himself who had to remind them about it.

"Oh, and I'd advise a double helping today," he said lightly. "Help settle the nerves."

When she heard that Kate felt a little series of tingles fanning out round the base of her skull. It came back to her now. "*If something ever happened to me, I want you to give up having the chocolate drink. And not tell anyone.*"

Jimmy took her parents into the front room to ask them questions and she was left alone to make the chocolate.

OK. She'd do it. For Jake, just because it was the last thing he'd asked her to do, however ridiculous, and if she didn't do it she had a superstitious feeling that she would be endangering the chances of his safe return. Even so, she felt foolish when she came into the front room, carrying the tray high so that no one could see that her cup was empty.

They were busy talking anyway and hardly acknowledged her presence until Uncle Jimmy had exhausted what little knowledge and ideas Stuart and Oona might have about Jake's disappearance and turned his attention to her. Had she seen any sign that her brother had been about to do something out of character?

She was so used to regarding the smiling, caring

Uncle Jimmy as their best friend that without thinking Kate at once opened out about what had worried her yesterday.

"Well ... he was a bit strange," she said.

"In what way?" Uncle Jimmy asked. "When?"

The questions were quick and sharp and it gave her pause.

"In the afternoon. I think he was just bored, mainly."

"In what way was he strange? Did he say anything?" Jimmy waited for her answer with acute attention. She didn't like it.

"It's just a brother-sister thing. I had the *feeling* he was a bit strange. That's all."

It was none of his business. It *had* been a brother-sister thing.

Stuart was let off work today. Jimmy had taken whole charge of their crisis, but there were two more callers at the house that morning. The first was the sergeant from the police station. He too was firm that they should speak in the living room. That was about the only thing he was firm about. A large man who seemed to be sweating even more than the weather required, Kate had often exchanged nods with him in the street. She had not realized what a complete Mr Plod he was. His favourite question was, "And at what time would that be?"

He was talking to Stuart now. Stuart was in a state and did not notice how stupid the sergeant was.

The sergeant asked effortfully, "And so you did not know that your son was not here until you awoke this morning?"

"No."

"And at what time would that be?"

"Around seven – the same time as my wife."

"What was it that you did then?"

"We called for him in the house. Looked all over. Then we went out to look for him outside. Kate and me."

The sergeant wrote in his notebook and looked up. "And at what time would that be?"

He was so careful in everything and he looked somehow nervous at the same time. Kate was sorry for the sergeant and stepped towards him. "Would you like a cup of tea?"

The polite question was a bombshell to the man. He looked up at the ceiling in the direction of the light fitting and was at a complete loss. Standing quite near him, Kate could see the notebook where he'd let it droop down.

He had written nothing. On the pages, his biro had made ragged lines, no more than that.

The impact this made on Kate caused her to take a step back. She covered it by turning quite naturally and going towards the kitchen. "I'll put the kettle on anyway."

She was glad just to get out of the room. This was so weird. And the light fitting was making those funny little sounds again. Well, it often did that... But what to make of the sergeant? Was it that he was only showing willing in order to comfort them? It was impossible to know what to think. *Something's wrong*, Jake had said.

After the sergeant had gone Uncle Jimmy brought in the next visitor almost at once. It was the famous Stevie Morrison, the disc jockey, carrying a portable tape recorder. Wonder of wonders, they'd won Family of the Week.

As Jake had told her they would.

Stevie Morrison had a look of Uncle Jimmy about him. Both men were in late middle age and had hair longer than you might expect at that time of life. They seemed to get on well, too, and did most of the talking both before and during the taped interview.

The disc jockey explained that although he'd been told they were not at all as normal this morning, the Happy Families award was still theirs. He said, in his Scots accent, "Mebbe it's now above all that you need something like this, when you're worried about a loved one."

During the brief interview he was sententiousness personified, especially in his closing words, spoken close up to the microphone with breathy sincerity.

"This is a loving, caring family who are naturally not at their best this morning, with the uncertainty about the whereabouts of their dear son, Jake. But it's going to be Awwl Right, because with folks like these there's such a spirit of mutual care in times of trouble that the Higgins family will only emerge the stronger."

It was a relief when he went too. Jimmy went with him, urging them all to rest. He said he'd look in on Dr Dunning for them and fix up some appointments for stress counselling and a supply of tranquillizers. His last words were, "Stevie Morrison's right. You're still a great wee family and if the worst came to the worst about Jake, well, you'd stick together all the more. But he's most likely gone adventuring somewhere. He'll turn up."

Jake did not turn up that morning. Stuart had no idea what to do with himself and Oona wandered the house fretfully. Once Kate heard her calling, "Have we got any sherry in the house? Don't we keep a little sherry somewhere?"

Nevertheless, Stuart and Oona did manage to rest, falling heavily and unattractively asleep in the living room. Kate was driven upstairs just by the sight of them lying there. How could they sleep at a time like this?

She couldn't. Her mind was … just getting sharper and sharper. It darted around like a crazed mosquito. A policeman who couldn't write? She had to remember what Jake had said to her in every detail. Something about the pylon… She thought about walking past it and out of town and even as the idea popped into her mind she felt a frisson of fear.

And then the pressure was relieved. She found she was thinking the old, warm, comforting thoughts about children. The knot in her stomach relaxed. It was going to be Awwl Right. Of course it was. Somehow.

And she was going to have the most beautiful babies.

Jake was a swimmer. What a welcome discovery that had been.

Not only that, but he knew three different strokes and by rotating them he had managed to get to the far bank of the loch. It was a close-run thing. Near crippled with exhaustion when he started the marathon swim, he was frozen to the marrow within a minute. No one could lift arms as heavy as his were, time after time, and his swimming became progressively less effective.

There were two directional aids. The building he had seen acted as his beacon and, in the first light of day, was revealed to be a late-Victorian edifice built after the style of one of the major London railway stations. It stood on a rise a long distance above the loch, while at the water's edge was a ramshackle boat house, a Gothic extravaganza that remained standing only by force of habit. It reached out into the water on unsteady posts and Jake floundered in under the beamed roof with the last of his strength. Had it not been there, he believed he would have drowned within a couple of metres of the shore. Then there was the matter of hauling himself up on to the slippery decking, and again it seemed death by water was his fate. He was so enfeebled, with hands of ice, so waterlogged and so cold that the effort was almost beyond him. Even when out of the water he shivered with such violence that he thought his refrigerated bones must surely break. A pile of elderly sails offered refuge and he crawled over to bury himself as deep as he could in the layers of stiff, coarse canvas.

He told himself he would go on in a minute or two. The big house would have telephones and ... he'd call the police...

And, still shivering, he fell asleep.

He woke to a drip of water on his face and the sound of a heavy bombardment of rain assaulting the frail roof. It was full daylight outside and had been for many hours and the wind gusted great buckets of rain across the loch. He was stiffer than the sails that covered him and hated his weakness in sleeping when his duty to Kate called for swift action. Searching for something with which to stop him getting any wetter than he was already, he found a ripped yellow oilskin in the second storey loft. It was not exactly a fashion statement, but it would do.

Keeping his head down against the rain he marched jerkily up the hill to the big house. His muscles were taking their time to get back into working order. A wall ran around the house here at the back and he followed it round to the main driveway and the façade of the building, which was the Cheviot Peregrine Hotel, a sign informed him. He got the hotel bit, at least, if only because of the stars and rosettes on the sign.

Jake paused, looking up at the imposing entrance at the top of a broad flight of stairs. All of a sudden it didn't seem so easy to walk in and use a phone, even now. The rain tore into his face and he lowered his head and stood there fearful and undecided.

He had slept, while all the time Kate needed him. Guilt forced his hand and he stepped forward.

A buzzing sound made him turn back into the sleeting rain – an engine noise that was about to get deeper and a lot closer.

This was like a bad dream. It was the black-clad night-rider from the castle and he was speeding up the road to the hotel.

Jake's despair was total. After all he'd been through, the guy was still right behind him. If he didn't want to be recognized he had to do something quickly.

He went up the stairs to the hotel at a run and the bad dream got worse. He skidded into the glossy-floored foyer and at once the man behind the reception desk darted round from behind it and came at Jake almost at a run.

Jake flinched. The man was tall, with a receding chin and a fussy manner. He said in an exasperated voice, "Callum Fraser?"

Jake mumbled, "Sorry?" and the man misunderstood his meaning.

"Well, better late than never. Tomorrow use the service entrance, will you? Come on."

It was as Callum Fraser that he was introduced to a junior porter, Rory, a twenty-year-old with a wide, acned face and sly eyes. Almost at once they were walking down a hall to the cloakrooms. With Sholto's warning in mind, that anyone he came upon might betray him to the Castle, he played along with the assumption that had been made about his identity. If he could only stay out of trouble his moment would come.

"So you're Donal's friend – that right?" Rory asked.

"Um, yes."

"Got a P45?"

"Not on me," Jake bluffed.

"Better bring it tomorrow. Or at least your card. I thought you'd be Scots."

"I would be if I could be, but I can't," Jake riposted neatly.

Through the back of the cloakroom were the staff changing rooms. Jake was handed dark trousers, shirt and striped waistcoat. "You can't wear those trainers!" Rory complained, and found him a pair of black plimsolls that belonged to someone else. "You'd better hope no one looks at your feet. Not that anyone will, with all the activity we've got going on here."

"Is there a phone I can use?"

"Forget it, pal, you're late getting here and you'll no be back tomorrow if they find you chatting away to your girl before you've even started."

Rory chatted away, telling him how the commotion in the hotel had been caused by a sudden influx of new guests, who had booked to stay only yesterday. Jake was only half listening because he'd remembered – you don't need to pay to call the emergency services. He'd be all right there, even with a payphone.

The black plimsolls were tight on his feet, which hurt by the time they came back to the reception desk for further orders. The man in the suit wasted no time. "One of you – take the order in the corner." He rushed off to the front door, where half a dozen men were entering the hotel. They were dressed in smart casual clothes and looked very fit, with a glossy sheen of health on their faces.

"It's a convention of physiotherapists," Rory explained. "Their other booking fell through. Right – it's a smoko for me. You get the order."

He handed Jake a small pad and a pen. Jake said, "But what – what do I do?"

"Just get them what they want from the bar or the kitchens. Note it down – and get a room number. That's the most important thing – even if you don't bring them the right drinks!"

And he exited to the cloakrooms. Jake sighed and walked to the back corner of the reception area, where tables and chairs were set for people just arrived or about to go somewhere. He prayed he wouldn't encounter the one-man posse who had the motorcycle.

The two patrons sat in the darkest corner, where a giant rubber plant bent down over them to offer a degree of privacy. One of the men at the table was a burly man in early middle age, with silver hair cut short to his head, and the other was … Dr Dunning.

It was a moment of jaw-dropping consternation. Dr Dunning – or, rather, Ralph Seton-Lindsay – who was on his way to buy pharmaceutical goods.

Or then again, maybe not.

At the moment of recognition Jake faced a choice and immediate flight was the one he favoured. Strongly. Curiosity and his forward momentum carried him on almost against his will, however, and he judged that by standing next to the rubber plant and averting his face a little, the man he'd known as his doctor would only have a limited view of him. He swept his hair the wrong way and made his voice sound hoarse when he attempted a touch of a Scots accent. It sounded laughable even to his own ears.

"Yaaissar?"

"Oh, there you are," said the burly man. He had a real American accent, which Jake placed as coming from somewhere in the south-west of that country.

"Yaaissar." The Seton-Lindsay man had turned his head to look at him and Jake began to stick his tongue in the side of his cheek by way of facial disguise, twisting his head further away.

The American ordered Scotch. "What else, huh – in Scotland? Straight. What's yours, Seton-Lindsay?"

"Still mineral water, please."

"OK," the American said, "Got that, boy?"

The magical phrase: "Yaaissar."

And the plan came to him even as he left their table, on his way to the bar.

Getting the drinks was no problem. He asked for extra slices of lemon for the mineral water and stuffed them into his cheeks on his way back with the tray. And hoped. He walked quietly in the black plimsolls and Seton-Lindsay was unaware of his approach. The doctor was saying, "The sprinkler system. It's so simple," and broke off as Jake reached his elbow, face averted.

"Suh." Lay the drinks down. Present the pad, keeping head bowed low over the table. "Saign thar, suh. And yer rheum naimber, please."

He saw Seton-Lindsay frown slightly at the strange accent, now rendered even more impenetrable by the lemon wedges, but the American seemed to have no trouble in following him. "There you go, boy." He wrote on the bill with a flourish and dropped a pound coin on top of it.

"Thunk yer suh."

Thank you, thank you – he'd got away with it! He was nearly running by the time he reached the reception desk, where the tall man was still dealing with the new arrivals and, being in quite a fluster, did not see Jake removing the fruit peel from his mouth.

"Excuse me – can I have the room key for forty-two? American gentleman wants his briefcase. Gave me a pound!"

"Yes, yes."

And he had the swipe card key and he was on his way to the lift.

Room forty-two was a double with a huge bed and an inter-connecting sitting room. Important guy, the American, then. Jake's idea was that if he and Seton-Lindsay were here on business then he, Jake, should get an idea of what that business was.

There was a phone by the bed. Great. First he should make that call. After reading the instructions he picked up the phone and dialled "nine" to get an outside line. A woman's voice said, "Good afternoon. What number do you require?" and he hung up. Later, then.

After the bad news, the good news. There was a real-life briefcase here...

And it was locked.

He found a ballpoint pen by the Welcome Pack the hotel put out for its guests, and tried jiggling it in the lock, with no success of course. But the case was of soft leather, so there were still possibilities. Nothing in the bathroom... Nothing in the sitting room... Jake's anxiety level was soaring because of the time this was taking. It was when he looked in the drawer of the bedside table that he found what he needed. Under the standard issue Gideon Bible there was a more unusual object: the American liked to keep a Bowie knife close to hand when he slept. It was broad and long and whetted sharp enough to cut through the breast-bone of a nocturnal assassin.

What kind of hotel guest had a knife like that?

The kind who didn't realize how very useful it would be in cutting open his own luxury leather case – and with some ease, at that.

Inside the briefcase were papers. The first Jake looked at was an Ordnance Survey map of the area. Yes – there was the body of water, which was called St Agnes' Loch, and the hotel … and Broomcleuch Castle. Well, the word started "Broom" and the graphic was of a castle…

More informatively, there was, too, a map of a castle and an inventory of men – some twenty in all – and their weapons. Jake could read few of these words but he recognized *10mm* and *small arms* and had a good guess at *fully automatic*.

A convention of physiotherapists? Armed and suddenly without a place to stay in? And Seton-Lindsay, at the same hotel?

You'd have to say it looked like the members of SCOM were about to be most unpleasantly surprised as they went about their routine tasks of … what was it? Ensuring the Continuance of Mankind?

Jake's hands were sweating. Kate was in even greater danger than he had guessed. All he needed was a public telephone – was it so much to ask?

He left the room as he'd found it and threw the ruined bag under the bed. That might buy him a little time, if the briefcase couldn't be found for a while. He dared not take its contents with him: too incriminating by half. He left the knife, as well, after remembering to wipe his fingerprints from it with a towel.

Back out into the corridor. The lift was busy, so take the stairs beside the shaft. Four floors down, round and down and down and round and out into the reception area near the cloakrooms. He could see the man at the desk and hear him too, in urgent conversation with Rory and another boy – a boy who wore very smart shiny shoes and who was very agitated.

"No – it's me, of course it's me!"

"Then in God's name who's that other boy?" the tall man asked in a shrill voice.

The other boy was the boy who did not fancy a scene in a hotel full of his enemies and who turned now and slipped into the corridor that led to the kitchens and the staff entrance by the car park. Once out of sight of the reception area Jake's smooth swift walk became a run.

The real Callum Fraser had come on a bike and it was somehow fitting that he should steal it.

Everything was going for him. There was no one watching and the rain had eased to a steady drizzle. Belt off and stop at the first phone he saw.

Except, as he tore along the empty road, going upwards, away from the loch and the Cheviot Peregrine Hotel, there were no telephones. Not even any houses. Only acre upon acre of rolling grassland. He topped the hill and the forsaken landscape was still unblemished by signs of human habitation. The road swept down though a forest, a good kilometre away, cutting through it, so at least there was cover to be found if a pursuit was made.

He twisted to look behind him and groaned aloud in disbelief at what he saw.

No doubt alerted by the excitement at the hotel, the motorbike was back on his tail.

10

The effect of seeing his nemesis caused instant wheel-wobble on the bicycle. Jake hung on to the handlebars, straightened the bike and stood up on the pedals, bearing down on them with all the force he could. Going downhill already, the bicycle's wheels raced so fast it felt as if his feet couldn't keep up with the whirling pedals, although he was in top gear. Even so, no cyclist on earth could outrun a motorcycle. Not on a road, anyway. He let his eyes flick from one side of the road to the other, where low banks held back the grasslands and he weighed up the options. How long had he got before he was headed off?

When you got to go, you got to go. He leaned over and turned the bike on to the roadside bank –

together they leapt a metre in the air and landed in a huge skid in the long damp grass. He was sensible enough to aim himself downhill still, and adept enough on a bike to steer into the skid and control it. What he hadn't reckoned on was the braking effect of the tall bleached grasses. Now he heard the bike – actually heard it vault the bank behind him, wheels clear off the ground – heard it slide – heard it wrenched back on course – and knew that he was done for. He wouldn't surrender without a fight and that meant choosing a suicidally steep route towards a blind drop that was coming up…

Now he was going fast enough. Too fast, his eyes weeping from the onrushing air – and again he was flying clear of the ground.

It is a matter of common sense to find sheltered sites when building in wild places. Jake landed on a muddy track leading to a small stone cottage and hurtled straight into the low drystone wall that surrounded it. The front wheel of the bike buckled and he flew over the handlebars like a circus acrobat, to land in a pond; or perhaps it was a deep puddle. Certainly it was strewn with sharp stones, and when he dragged himself to his feet he was bleeding from a cut on the forehead.

He limped muddily to the two-part door and knocked wildly on the upper section. "I need the police!" he shouted. "Someone help – please!" He twisted his head and looked. The motorcyclist had come to a stop at the top of the rise. He waited, so sinister in the black clothes.

A scraping sound – the top part of the door opened. "Please help," Jake said, even before he saw who was answering his appeal.

What he saw was so reassuring he could have kissed it. A broad, rosy face under soft grey hair tied up in a bun, a floral print dress, the kindly eyes of a farmer's wife straight from central casting. The motherly eyes widened in concern at the sight of him.

"I need help – please!" Jake spluttered.

"I can see that!"

"And the police – have you got a phone?"

He twisted his head to see and the rider picked that moment to turn his bike and ride off whence they had come with a snarl from the motorcycle that seemed to express his frustration.

The woman was speaking. "You come on in. First things first." She turned to call as she opened up the lower part of the door: "Robbie!"

Two minutes later Jake was seated in a warm kitchen with a slice of cake and a cup of sickeningly sweet tea. Robbie bent over him, bandaging his head. The farmer was a craggy man who said nothing at all.

"The telephone?" Jake asked. "I, er, I was being chased. I've got to phone the police." He thought it wiser not to go into any greater detail about his circumstances. Just make that one call and Kate could be saved.

"A telephone. Well now – did you see any telegraph poles when you came rushing down here?" She was teasing. "We have a mobile somewhere. Yes – somewhere... Got a mind of its own, like those things you point at the television."

"Thanks."

"I'll go and have a look, shall I?" She went out of the room and Jake was left with the Trappist farmer, who had just finished tying a perfect knot to secure the bandage when there came a shrill squealing from outside, making Jake start.

The man said in a harsh voice, "Sow. Farrowing," and immediately exited the kitchen through the back door with something approaching enthusiasm.

When Jake got to his feet his legs wobbled to tell him they wanted no more excitement today. Quietly, he made them take him into the narrow hall. He was going to check that the rider had well and truly gone – until he heard the soft, friendly voice of the farmer's wife, from upstairs.

The gentle voice was saying, "Yes – Sir William, please. Will you tell him we have the lad he was looking for and can he get some men here quickly?"

So Sholto had been right – and he had chosen the wrong house in which to seek assistance.

Precipitous action was second nature to Jake by now and he moved swiftly to the front door – which the rosy-cheeked woman had bolted tightly: both halves. It did not take long to unlock the upper section but it was a noisy business so he forgot about the lower part and threw himself out bodily. His legs still protested, but not as much as the farmer's wife as she scrambled down the stairs.

"You – boy – don't go! I've got more cake – sausages! ROBBIE! Get the gun!"

Pigs came first, maybe. In all events, Jake was running – downhill for the usual reasons of speed – fast enough to put a good distance between himself and the cottage by the time Robbie emerged with a cheap but serviceable shotgun. The spread of the shot at this range rendered the scatter-gun useless, but Robbie fired all the same, obeying his warm and wonderful wife in all matters.

They were too old to contemplate a pursuit on foot, yet possessed, as well as a pregnant pig, a motorcycle of their own with a dented sidecar in which Mrs Robbie rode in state. Once again this took time to organize and meanwhile Jake had hit a small road which meandered round to enter the far-off forest – he guessed. Well, he'd never get that far... In the other direction was a small stand of trees that wasn't nearly big enough to hide in for more than a second or two. What to do?

Two engines coughed into life. Away up by the cottage Robbie had at last managed to kick-start his old war-horse while, in the small copse where he had been waiting, the night-rider had used the electrical ignition on his machine to bring it to life in an instant. He roared up out of the trees and when Jake saw him he sank to his knees in the middle of the road.

Defeated. Everything he'd done was in vain. No phone call.

No future for Kate.

The black motorbike sped up to him and slammed to a stop.

"What is it wiv you?" a severe voice asked. Jake raised his head. The helmet was off and under it was a smooth golden face with black olive pit eyes. "Why are you always running?"

The young man was Japanese and he spoke with an accent that combined Tokyo with California.

"What?" Jake asked dully. The Japanese youth glanced up to view the old motorcycle and sidecar beginning its lumbering chase.

"Get on," ordered the owner of the scramble bike. "Let's go talk somewhere."

A feeling of safety abruptly swept over Jake. Wordlessly, he mounted the bike at the back and held on to the leather jacket of its rider.

They accelerated away in the direction of the great forest, leaving Mr and Mrs Robbie trailing far behind but motoring on gamely all the same.

The suffocating heat of the day was really getting to

her. She'd never felt so claustrophobic, wandering the house and worrying.

It was worse when her parents were up and about again. Stuart talked bravely about going on as usual, yet things weren't as usual. Oona was getting splitting headaches and it seemed that Dr Dunning was away on a short holiday and there were no other doctors available. She had something unbalanced about her today that had nothing to do with her migraines. Like when she said – the first part, at least, making sense – "He could have phoned. I hope he's got enough carrier bags with him."

It was time to put Jake's theory to the test. She'd put it off long enough. Kate said, "I'm going out for some fresh air."

Outside the front door the sun beat down on to her auburn hair and at once she was uncomfortably warm. Air, maybe, but it wasn't so fresh. Perhaps she should wander down into town instead and walk into some supermarket with that chilly air-conditioning they had in such places.

She didn't, though. Her feet took her up to the recreation strip.

A driver was loading cardboard boxes into a van outside Taylor's. "Phew," he said. "Another scorcher."

His shirt bulged out behind as if he was smuggling a heavy load of vegetables out of his place of work. Or maybe there was something wrong with his lower back. He moved awkwardly too, and his slack jaw hung wide open like that of a panting animal. Kate found she was staring at him; they were locked in eye contact and it was embarrassing for both of them. "A real…" he fumbled for some apposite word, "*scorcher*," he said, as if by saying the word with more emphasis it gave it a wholly different meaning.

It was enough to break the moment. "Yes," she agreed politely, and left him to his work. She heard the van door shut and he passed her, motoring at a snail's pace up the hill and out of town.

Where she was going.

Where she wasn't.

Where she *was*, because she was a free agent and she could do what she liked.

She couldn't even get beyond the police station.

Her worry sharpened to outright fear and she wheeled away to go home.

Mr Roche was standing by the Rec. He waited for her to approach and fell into step beside her. "Kate!" he said heartily. "Well now! You look a bit glum!" His refined voice was so confident it got under her skin.

"Yes," she agreed.

"Yes… You're worried about your brother. We've all heard about it. I've got a brother you know, and I do understand what it's like to be worried about someone you care for. But, you know, Kate, you'll get through this all right. You must never under-estimate the resilience of the human spirit. Never underestimate yourself, if it comes to that. I'm sure young Jake will be all right, wherever he is."

"Well, maybe."

He put a bony hand on her shoulder. "It's the most awful thing, to live with uncertainty." He was looking at her very intently. "How do you *feel*?"

It was like a critical question in an oral exam. She was at once cautious, though she didn't let it show.

"I feel fine."

"That's the ticket. I'll look in from time to time. If that's all right."

"Yeah – do." She wished he'd take his hand off her shoulder. He did, after giving it a little squeeze.

"Brave girl."

Outside her house he stopped, beaming at her.

"You're a very special person. You know that?"

She suspected he wanted her to invite him in. Well, she wouldn't. To make that quite plain she strolled on down the hill a few paces. When she looked back, Mr Roche had been nabbed by the Bartons, who must have been hovering at the window just waiting to drag him in for a cup of tea. The ghastly neighbours fawned on the postman in the most sycophantic way, squirming with gratification at the honour he was about to do them. Sickening. And sort of odd, because they didn't actually say anything.

What was happening to her? Even the people in the street looked different today. Or perhaps she was only seeing things with a new clarity – she was so much more together than she'd been since … since she couldn't remember when. Did *all* the locals look different, or had something changed? Here came a couple on their way up to Taylor's, a pair in their mid-twenties and – should they be out in that condition? Shouldn't they see a doctor? If they could find one, that was.

They were bent over as they walked, in the grip, it would seem, of excruciating stomach pains. Their faces were contorted with the effort of walking, which was something they did very slowly. Mindful of their manners, they glanced over at Kate and spoke.

"Lovely … lovely…" the young man gasped.

"*Day*," his companion finished for him.

She had stopped just past the post office. Suddenly Billy Smith was at her elbow.

"Kate."

" 'Lo, Billy."

"So … what have you been up to?"

"Nothing," Kate answered swiftly, with that caution springing to the fore again.

His narrow face was close; his eyes very penetrative. "I meant, have you just been for a walk or something."

"Oh – yes."

"I could have come with you. Next time, just let me know."

"Yeah, right."

She nudged past him to get to her own front door. He said, "Kate," and it stopped her.

"What."

"I'm your friend. I like you Kate. Now things have changed and you'll need a friend."

"Nothing's changed. Jake'll be back soon."

"Well…"

A coughing, honking sound made him turn from her to the factory. On the forecourt two workers were doubled over in pain, watched passively by one of their mates. One of the men fell sideways to the ground, stiff as a board.

"Excuse me. Catch you later," Billy said, and ran over to the men.

"Maybe."

But he hadn't heard.

Utterridge Forest was big. Icky (who would want to be called *that*?) had left the road and steered the lightweight motorcycle cautiously through the tall trees, with the occasional judder as they hit roots under the soft forest floor. Now they sat in the cathedral-like arboreal gloom, which was illuminated only by a pencil torch with remarkably good battery life.

"KK deep cell battery – best you can buy," the

Japanese youth had announced gnomically. He was twenty-three years old and named Icky, or, more properly, Ichimura Kankuro. And he shone silver in the forest, as did Jake. Icky had produced from his panniers two big squares of what looked like aluminium foil which he had pronounced to be "Microlight Thermal Permafrost Blankets", and which both had draped around themselves against the cold. Other than the moment when Icky had introduced himself rather stiffly, there had been no real talk until now.

"OK," he said quietly, "here we are. Who goes first? Who are we?"

"Yeah, well ... the thing is, I'm not quite sure ... I'm Jake Higgins, as far as I've been told, but I don't think it's true."

Icky pondered that one. "Interesting. Now then, I fink you were getting away from Broomcleuch Castle – yes?"

His English was remarkably good and only now and then did you get a consonant that betrayed his Oriental origins.

"And I think you've been watching the castle," Jake answered him.

They were fencing with each other so far. "Look at this." Icky produced a grainy black and white photograph. The definition was quite good enough for Jake to make out that it was a picture of himself, just out of the courtyard when leaving the castle.

"Infra-red polaroid telephoto. And all that night there was a big commotion. Search parties. Looking for you?"

"Should think so."

"Yeah. I had to get out of Blackhope Tower in a hurry. Very, very exciting."

"Blackhope Tower?"

"Yeah. The old square Pele Tower. My advanced operations base round here. You'd have gone past it. Tried to find you, but I lost you."

"Pele Tower?"

"Sure. Don't you know anything about this part of Scotland?"

"I don't know anything about any part of Scotland."

Icky shook his head in wonder. "Very very great part of the British Isles. Close by Dumfries and Galloway where Mr John Buchan, Lord Tweedsmuir, set much of his famous adventure-spy story *The Thirty-Nine Steps*. You've read it of course. Richard Hannay – great action hero, armed only with stout walking boots, revolver and binoculars and sometimes not all three at once."

"I don't read."

"I thought everyone here read John Buchan."

"Not me, anyway."

Icky appeared to change the topic of conversation. "When my father sent me here I was real happy to come. The place in the West I most wanted to see.

Beats the hell out of Santa Barbara. Now I find I'm some kind of Richard Hannay myself, only more high-tech. You have to tell me what gives in Broomcleuch Castle."

"Why?" Jake asked plainly.

Ichimora Kankuro considered. "OK. This is how it is. My father is Kawatake Kankuro. KK Industries."

Jake saw he was meant to be impressed. "Never heard of him."

"You don't know much about anything, do you? Not even yourself," the Japanese responded sourly. "He's a big man wiv big ideas. Spreads himself wide. There's this Sir William Carrick-Boyd over here and he's researching worker compliance. This is getting important in Japan. My father funds his research, along with a whole load of other multi-nationals. We don't get much back and so I'm sent to see what gives. I been staying at the Peregrine Hotel. Only found you again by chance."

Jake was getting interested. "And what does give?"

"Sir William takes me round the labs and tries to tell me they're developing drugs that can improve work-rate and provide increased passivity. Research still in the early stages. But I'm not stupid."

"It's something to do with breeding a better race", Jake said slowly, "only it goes wrong, I think."

"You're telling me. I found something before they kicked me out."

Letting his Thermal Permafrost Blanket fall, he went to his bike and delved deep into one of the panniers. "In the corner of one of the labs. Picked something up. It didn't feel right. My dad says, 'Keep watching. Learn more.' 'Cos it could be his reputation's at stake here."

"He's got nothing to do with all those blokes at the big hotel?"

"No. And that's something else – those guys."

"I need to call the police."

"No way. That's one reason I wanted to get to you – I don't want my father's name tarnished. He's a great man."

"Those men at the hotel. They're going to break into the Castle and they're armed. That's one of the things I do know. Now what about the police?"

Icky came back from the bike with a small tin which he passed to Jake. "Could be they are the police, of one kind or another. Ever think of that?"

"No…"

As Jake opened the tin Icky shone his torch on it. "This is real big stuff. Take look."

"What is it?" All Jake could see was that it seemed to be a small animal.

Icky plucked it from the tin and held it up in the torchlight. "It's a mouse. Of a kind. It was dead. Must have crawled into a corner to die and I don't blame it."

Yes, it was a mouse. Mainly. For it had six black

crooked legs and its eyes were huge and bulbous and meshed like kitchen sieves.

Jake gulped back something bitter that had risen into his throat. "There's people down under the castle who've got legs like that."

"Is that right? Well, I got good grades in biology and I can tell you something."

"What?" Jake asked, both knowing and dreading the answer.

"They're insect legs."

11

Later in the afternoon they gave up trying to watch videos and opted for a soothing cup of tea. In the kitchen Stuart suddenly rammed his fist into the door with a furious brutality that shocked Kate, who retreated to her room. Of course, he was venting his helplessness and resulting anger on an inanimate object – she understood his motives, but it was an unpleasant episode.

As a mother, Oona felt Jake's absence terribly. Coming back to her in the kitchen for a hug, Kate found her on her hands and knees searching for something under the sink. She craned her head round at her daughter and said, "Every house has a drop of cooking sherry somewhere. Or something left over from Christmas."

The wheels were coming off around here and Kate had never felt so alone. Where was Jake? Who could she trust? She wished he was with her.

She didn't know what to *do*.

For all that they talked for many minutes, even hours, neither Jake nor Ichimura advanced very far their understanding of what was going on at Broomcleuch, even after Jake had come clean about all he knew. Icky was enthralled at the idea of some kind of breeding programme. It was different for Jake, because it was going to happen to the person he cared most about in the world, and it was for differing reasons that they intended to get back into the Castle before anything happened to it. With his father's interests in mind, Icky's plan was to get a photographic record of whatever was going on – while it still *was* going on – and Jake just wanted to get Kate out and away before they were parted by events beyond their control.

Frustratingly, despite his role as man of action, the Japanese youth would not be persuaded to make an immediate move. "These guys booked into a hotel. You do that if you're spending the night there – right? So they're not taking action till tomorrow at the earliest, is my guess. Probably won't even be in a position to."

"You don't think that when that bloke finds his briefcase all slit open he might get things moving a little quicker?"

"It's a possibility. But, any case, they aren't going to want to march up to someone else's castle till the wee small hours, if that's what they're here to do," Icky pronounced authoritatively, if quaintly. "So give it some hours and under the cloak of night we got a real good chance to get there first and get in when everyone's asleep. I can't see any other way of entering and exiting again without a barrel-load of trouble."

He had climbing equipment stored in Blackhope Tower, along with many other items he regarded as essential for the self-respecting independent secret agent. Such things as the K-rations he produced for their sustenance: dried foods and high-glucose drinks, all of which Jake found to have a very Japanese kind of taste, bland and sticky.

Icky himself was not at all bland when he discovered that his mobile phone was suffering interference so deep in the woodland and he could not reach his father in Tokyo. Instead he jumped up and down and swore mightily. He tried again at intervals, with the same lack of success and resulting Japanese bad language. It was while he was engaged in such imprecations for the third or fourth time that Jake held up a hand.

"Wait – stop."

"What – what?"

"Listen."

Vehicles. Several of them, by the sound of it.

Travelling through the forest. Coming from the direction of the hotel. On a route all the way round the loch – going to the Castle? Only, now the engines slowed. And cut out.

Icky expressed it. "What's happening here? What do we do?"

"Dunno," Jake said cautiously. Recent experience suggested to him that discretion was an undervalued option, but for Icky, super-spy, this vehicular enigma was good news. Something to do.

"I'll go take a look. You stay here. No point to take a chance with bofe of us."

He set off with a careful step, excited and already on the lookout for danger, his eyes darting this way and that. Within moments his slight figure was lost in the darkness.

Once he had gone, Jake's wariness seemed to him not only uncourageous but silly too. Now what he was doing was waiting and that was an activity he'd had too much of when he was with Sholto. Fortunately, before he'd had time to get himself really tense the Japanese was back with him. "Gonna take the camera. Get a record of everything," he whispered.

"What's up, then?"

"Men from the hotel, meeting up with their transport. Four wheel drive stuff." Icky added with pride, "Japanese-made, naturarry."

"I'll come with you."

"No – no. They got guns, just like you said. Two of us too risky. Make too much noise. This is my area of excellence. But – hey – you were right – it's tonight! You stay, be ready to move fast."

Being right was all very well; being inactive was another. Left to his own devices again, Jake went over to the motorbike and sat on it, working the throttle and pressing on the brakes. What if Icky didn't make it back? Should he take this and move on? Could he make it work in the first place? He tried to recall what Icky did when he was on the bike. He got off it, thought of rummaging for more food in the panniers…

And heard shots fired.

He wasn't sure at first. They didn't sound like they did in the movies. Lighter, sharper. When he heard Icky crashing back to him through the undergrowth and the bullets whirring by at high velocity, ripping through leaves and branches, he was convinced. He dashed to the bike and turned the key in the ignition. The engine jumped into action. Now what? Automatic fire whistled past his head – you could sense the weight of the bullets from the breeze that snapped at his ear. Then Icky was with him and leaping on to the back of the bike with a force that almost brought them to the ground. Twist the throttle and the automatic gears engaged and the wheels spun and there was a thump and Icky held on to him tightly and then there was a metallic *ting* –

and they were away, slewing through the fallen leaves and falling first right and then left and picking up speed until it was pure instinct that kept him from smashing into the broad tree trunks. He discovered that his reflexes were ahead of his mind; it was like being a passenger in his own body – you sensed the obstacles and the bike was a part of you, responding to your needs of the moment.

The snarl of the motorcycle engine in the still night made it impossible to tell if they were being fired on, or if any chase was being made at all. Once he was going, though, Jake kept going. As he rode, a strong smell of petrol gusted into his nose. After about five minutes of furious travel, dodging every which way through the obstacles, paler light between the trees indicated that they were about to charge out of the forest. Jake kept right on. Better to be travelling fast if there was anyone waiting for them. He had lost all sense of direction in the trees and as the trees thinned he was glad to see a wide shimmer of water, which he took to be St Agnes' Loch. He would have some idea of where they were.

It was freezing cold. They left the trees and jounced across the moorland and he became aware that Icky's grip on his waist was loosening – his passenger was sliding around like a string bag of satsumas. The sudden changes of gravity at his rear were making it impossible for Jake to control the bike. He wound down the throttle until he was in second gear and as he reached a speed that could be considered a crawl by his previous standards, Icky fell from the bike, a dead weight.

In gravitational sympathy with its owner, the bike fell as well. It was too light to do Jake much damage and he quickly extricated himself from under it without stopping to check his own bruised body, too worried about Icky.

Ichimura Kankuro lay on his belly, half-hidden in the long grass in the freezing dew, his face turned to one side, eyes shut as though in sleep. Jake turned him over. It took some effort and the dew on Icky had become warm. And sticky...

He'd been shot. The lower right-hand side of his torso had leaked out blood. He was breathing, so he was alive, and that was the extent of the good news.

Jake went back to the bike and hauled it up and stood it on its stand. The smell of petrol was very strong. On himself, too. The bike had been hit: there was a neat round hole in the tank. Oh, this was just getting better and better. In the panniers ... there must be something in them that would be of use in this situation.

Some minutes later he knew there wasn't. Small strips of elastoplast were no good to Icky and they wouldn't adhere to petrol soaked metal, either, so they were doubly useless. In desperation, he turned to the mobile phone. Not only had he never worked one of these before, as far as he knew, but when the

148

display came on it was unreadable – and not just to a dyslexic. It was in Japanese. He tried to navigate the menu all the same, with predictably negative results. Reduced to pressing buttons in every combination he could think up, he reached three numbers. On each occasion the person that answered was Japanese; one a young man, the other two, women. The man on the line used a stern quick voice that panicked Jake, who said into the telephone: "Icky. Ichim – Ichimure … Icky. Icky's hurt. In trouble."

The young Japanese man spat out a series of questions and Jake answered with, "Icky's in trouble. In Scotland."

The man apparently became very angry when Jake would not speak Japanese and Jake hung up on him.

The women were gentler but spoke no English either and one of them became quite hysterical. Jake told them in English that Icky was in trouble and cut the line.

It wasn't just Icky who was in trouble, of course, and it was getting worse. Headlights were cutting through the night sky. At least five sets. Three from one end of the woodland and two from the other. The lights bounced and wavered; the vehicles were off-road. It didn't take a genius to work out that the quasi-military force had divided in search of the motorcycle. And would soon find it. Jake ran back to Icky. He didn't want to leave him here but with or without him he was on his way and soon.

He took hold of Icky's shoulder. "Wake up!" he shouted, "Wake *up*!"

The furious order had an effect. Icky stirred and said faintly, "Why?"

"We've got to move."

"I been shot."

"I know."

Icky managed to raise himself on to one elbow. "They don't use expanding bullets. Or the ones that turn over in the air. That's something." He explained lucidly, "It's my side. Fink it went straight through. Only clipped me."

"Yes." If he was showing off his action-man knowledge again he couldn't be too badly hurt, Jake supposed. "We've got to move on. They're coming."

"Yeah. We got get to Blackhope Tower. I got medical supplies there – everything. We got to move."

But he didn't. It took a lot of manhandling to get him to the bike and when he got on he was limp and bendy.

Well, see how we go.

"Hang on," Jake said tersely and started the engine. This was marvellous. Within hours of finding Icky his ally had already become a burden.

It was a relief to be under way again. He drove down to the waterside, in that way gaining maximum distance on the two-part posse. It appeared that Icky was able to cope with the bumpy ride, at least so far. They were going to have to work their way all the way round the loch. Jake hoped they'd have enough fuel to get to the tower. And then? he'd leave Icky – having done what he could for him – and go on for Kate.

It was still the thought of Kate that motivated him. It was always Kate. He had to look after her, had to save her from the underground town. Had to. And he would.

Icky was slumping again. Jake stopped the bike to wake him up and re-focus him. He had not used the bike's headlights, naturally, and was reassured to see that there were no other headlights visible now. Reassured at first, anyway.

Icky said weakly, "They gone?"

"Looks that way."

"They should have night-sight gear. Maybe even heat detectors," Icky said helpfully, in a rambling kind of way. "You want to leave me here?"

"No."

Then he heard the motors. They'd cut their lights, maybe so as not to disturb the few local people asleep in their beds, or maybe for other reasons of stealth, but they were still coming.

"You hold on really tight," Jake told Icky and they took off again.

Round the loch, mile by mile, and the land rose upwards. It was not a bright night and Jake wondered if they'd even find the tower. He had to guess at what point to abandon the loch and strike out for the direction of the castle. There was a sense of security in travelling uphill when he did at last make the decision. They must be going at least roughly in the right direction. Now the engine was spluttering. Perhaps they were running on fumes alone. Out in the middle of nowhere, feeling very alone, only not as alone as they would have wished to be.

When they came to the crevasse he stopped just in time. They had hit a ravine that traversed the countryside, appearing and disappearing at haphazard intervals. Though he didn't know it, the split in the land was part of the geological fault line that ran under Broomcleuch. What he did know was that there was no way over it. He was preparing to turn the bike to skirt along the rocky downfall until there was a safe way over, when the searchlight came on.

The jeeps were pretty close behind them. Only a third of a kilometre below. Gaining speed, if the big light on one of them was an indicator. Coming up fast. *They'd have a map – they'd know they had him trapped.*

"Why we stopped?" Icky mumbled, still clutching on to him.

"We haven't. Hold on tighter than ever."

To make the jump he had to turn the bike and go back. Towards the jeeps. The big light caught and held them and he was dazzled as he again turned the bike and wound the throttle full up.

A wonder of Japanese engineering, the rough-terrain machine bounded up towards the ravine with alacrity.

It could have been as a consequence of asking for maximum power, but the overheated engine finally accepted an unfortunate law of physics and produced a flickering finger of flame. The flame grew. Jake didn't know if it was burning him or not – the vital thing was that they were going fast enough, weren't they? The ravine wasn't *that* wide, surely. Only, they were going uphill … and … they'd make it.

Or would they? The bike hit a rock and jumped before he wanted it to. They were in mid-air, flying above a deep drop into death, about to fall … and then the front wheel hit the other side of the crevasse and the rear wheel followed and the ravine didn't get them.

The other one did – the twin fissure just beyond its brother; the one he couldn't see because their journey was uphill. More grass-padded, not as deep, not as dangerous – but deep enough. Icky came off the bike one side as they tumbled down and he came off the other and the bike preceded them down into the narrow burn below and exploded into a red hot inferno of fire.

This cleft in the land was so much more friendly than the first. Jake survived the fall. He crawled to where Icky lay. The conflagration was being controlled by the water at the bottom of the gully, reduced to a small metal bonfire now, and dwindling fast; they must have exhausted all but the last drops of petrol by the time their journey had ceased.

Heat seeking devices? Dazed and numb, Jake dragged Icky's unresisting body into the freezing water and lay in it with him. He felt almost sleepy. It was shock, no doubt. If he actually fell asleep they'd die of exposure. If Icky wasn't dead already. If someone didn't reach them first and speed up the process.

There was no Jake on the other side of the partition. She was alone in the smothering heat of the night. Kate couldn't sleep.

Before they'd gone to bed the policeman had called again, though only to tell them there was no news of Jake. She wouldn't have believed him even if he had something to tell them. He was a fake.

She turned over in bed for the hundredth time. Went on to her back again. She did miss Jake, so much. He had always been … *right there*.

Her busy mind threw up a random memory. It was very hazy, but there had been a boy and he had let her down. They had been running away to London and he'd taken all their money to go and get food and he'd never come back. Just for a second she could see it – night, rain and nowhere to shelter, cars speeding past … and a plump blond boy called … no – she couldn't remember his name. He was terrible. She hated him.

What had all that dreaming about marriage been about? She wasn't interested – not one bit. And if she had been running away with a boy, then when could that have happened? Not so very long ago. Couldn't have.

She turned over again. *Oh, please, please, let me get some SLEEP!* She was positive now Jake had been abducted. She'd have to tell her parents everything in the morning. Just have to. Whatever the consequences. She couldn't go on feeling this alone and frightened.

Wait. What was that? Footsteps on the stairs. She sat up at once. The steps were slow and quiet. It was someone *creeping* up the stairway … someone, surely, who could only be Jake, returned, feeling guilty about worrying them and coming to her first. Oh thank God, thank God.

She was all ready to say, "Jake," when the intruder appeared in the doorway.

It was her father.

Carrying a carving knife. It glinted in the faint light from the street. Kate was too astonished to speak. Wearing his striped cotton pyjamas, Stuart came towards her bed, still using that elaborate sneaking step she'd heard on the stairs, though he must have seen her sitting there staring at him. Mustn't he?

One long, surreptitious step at a time he came to her side. He spread his arms a little in a defence-attack posture, with the knife held back some way by his hip. Kate now saw that his eyes were glazed and his mouth hung open. He was sleepwalking, perhaps, or under the malign influence of – what? Stress? Chocolate? What power on earth could turn her own dear father into this zombie?

It didn't look like Stuart at all. But it was Stuart. Her father.

And he had come to kill her.

12

Stuart shambled ever closer with the long knife, swaying in a trance-like stupor. Kate wouldn't – couldn't – use her voice to stop him, fearing that if she did he would sharpen up his act and move faster. When he raised the knife slowly, looking down on her with his eyes devoid of life, she threw back the covers and rolled out of bed. Her long nightdress hampered her terribly – acting as a stop-start cotton brake as she crawled along down by the bedside. He was turning slowly to locate her again. She stood up and ran for the door and his loud voice came after her. And he did, too.

"Hey – hinny – where you going?"

He'd never called her that. Nor "girlie".

"Girlie – you get back here!"

It sounded like he was awake now and sounded, too, as if his intentions hadn't altered. Kate didn't want to get trapped up here on the first floor and went down the stairs in a jumble of missed steps, bouncing off the wall as she went.

Then she turned back to look. Stuart was at the stop of the stairs, knife raised. His shouting had roused Oona who had come to his side. "Stuart, my darling," she said, "what are you doing up at this hour?"

She was still dazed from sleep. Stuart reacted to her as though they were having a normal conversation, growling, "Hush, woman – I'm after the little tramp there."

Oona came to. "No. No – Stuart – what are you doing – you're mad!"

He pushed at her with the hand that did not hold the knife. She held on to his arm.

"Stuart – !"

"Let me be, you – !"

And in a second they were struggling and in one more second they fell down the stairs, crashing head-long towards Kate in a flailing mass of body parts.

Kate was on the move before they hit the bottom. She couldn't stay here any longer: she flipped the lock on the front door and wrenched it open and fell out of the house into the hot embrace of the night. Whirling round immediately, she slammed the door and leaned into it, her chest heaving with the need to take in air. The intertwined bodies had landed on the hall carpet and there was a momentary silence. A light came on upstairs in the Barton's house as Kate listened to the silence and the sound of her own breathing. Perhaps the knife had found a target on the way down. Then her parents started shouting and whining at one another, in pain and shock and in the manner of a regular domestic dispute.

She would leave them to it. It was so good to be out here and not in there. That house was like a prison and she seemed to have been locked up in it for ever.

It was with a feeling of liberation that she turned away. And bumped into someone.

"Kate," he said.

Billy.

His narrow eyes pierced into hers. "What are you doing, Kate?"

"I – nothing. None of your business."

He asked, gently curious, "Why don't you drink the chocolate any more?"

A tiny pause – and Kate ran for it. Past the doctor's surgery and down towards the town. Running from the nightmare her life had become and running into another nightmare. Round the corner from the surgery and the flour factory she flew and tiny street lights shone from the town beneath. The bright lights of civilization. Except that ... the road had ended. Beyond the surgery it broadened and became a large parking area she had no knowledge of. The big asphalted space was empty. She slowed, trying to get her bearings. Lots of little lights in the sky ahead, and to her left a couple of lights from the flats ... but no road. Nowhere to go. She heard Billy jogging up softly behind her, in no great hurry. Kate took off again and ran blindly towards where the town should be if it was there at all and her pursuer's pace increased too in a rush and then she was pounced on, was being held back by Billy, whose strength was greater than seemed likely for his thin build. He said quietly, "There's no town. It's a big screen. A translucent material, with lights shining through. Touch it and you'll set off the sensors."

"Let go of me!" she said furiously.

And he did. "There's nowhere to go, Kate. This is all there is."

Kate stepped back from him and they faced each other, standing in the middle of the deserted car park. She said slowly, "What is this place?"

"This is the end of the world. Well, it's the end of your world, anyway."

"Where *are* we?" she asked desperately.

"We're in my world. I'll show you."

"No. Just tell me where we are *now*."

He was patient with her. "We're in one of the vehicle bays. All the cars and vans – and the bus you see going by – they're in the other one, at the back of the police station. Where they always finish up at the end of the day."

"This isn't true. You're lying."

He said, "When he goes to work, your dad just comes in through the back entrance of the surgery. He's programmed to think he's gone into town, but he never makes it."

"You're trying to trick me somehow."

"No. You've been trying to trick me. I've seen you in your living room, with a cup with nothing in it. You've stopped taking the sedatives – why?"

"You look through the window?" She was horrified.

He disregarded her question. "Listen. Your mum and dad. They haven't been behaving like your parents today – right?"

"Yes. No – whatever."

"Yeah, well, it's because they're not your parents."

Kate's legs weren't functioning at all well. She sank to her knees. "I don't know what's going on."

He came and squatted down beside her and said amicably, "Stuart was on the loose after he broke out of a psychiatric ward in Glasgow. He's got a history of violent behaviour. Oona was found on the streets of Aberdeen – alcoholic, with a lot of carrier bags and no friends. That's not their real names, of course."

"Jake," she said and looked at Billy full on. "If that's what they are, what's Jake?"

"A runaway." Billy couldn't hide his sudden anger and his dislike of Jake. "A nobody. Not your brother."

"Not my brother."

"Taken from the south coast of England. By the man you think of as Uncle Jimmy, who also found you after you went off with your boyfriend who left you on a motorway somewhere near Reading." He thrust his head closer to her. "Now where's Jake? Did he tell you where he was going? Did he tell you anything he knew?"

"No. Well…" Why not be honest about it? "He did leave a note about the chocolate."

"Yes? Did he? I'll tell you something else he left. He left instant concrete powder in the flour sacks and people are dying because of it. He didn't tell you that, did he?" Now Billy was not just angry, but savage.

"What people?"

"My people. Come on."

In getting to his feet he pulled her up with him. His strength really was alarming.

"Where are we going."

"I want you to see something."

"What?"

They were walking now, his hand gripping her just above the elbow. They went up to where the car park became the street. He said tenderly, "It's nice, being with you. I knew it'd be nice."

There was a man outside the factory. A worker with a terrible handicap – one of his eyes appeared to be permanently shut and the other was larger than it should be and resembled a bulging round teabag. All around it the bone structure of his face was raised in a big bump and the strangely grey, porous-looking eye stuck out even farther. The worker saw well enough through it, saying with shy adoration, " 'Lo, Billy."

"Hi," Billy answered briefly.

Ahead of them now were two policeman walking straight at them. Was there hope there? One of them said, "Hello." A single word, but it conveyed a respectful admiration for her companion.

Billy went on up the street with Kate. Her house and that of the Bartons were both showing lights through the curtains. She said, "I don't want to go back in there."

"That's not where I'm taking you. You might wish it was – later," he said, and they walked on up to Taylor's Fresh Produce, which was amazingly easy to get into. You just pushed open the door on the main greenhouse and went in and then you wondered why it was called Taylor's Fresh Produce because the sweet smell of rotting fruit and vegetation went direct to your stomach without passing "Go". It was dark in the glasshouse and there were indeed plants growing here – tomatoes, Kate guessed. She couldn't imagine, however, why they seemed to be walking on broken nut shells. The sounds of crunching and cracking had nothing to do with rotting fruit and once or twice it felt to her as if the whole floor was moving under her feet. Billy was still gripping her arm and, in spite of her negative feelings for him, she was holding on to him pretty tight too, now. It certainly was a large greenhouse, this one, she suddenly realized. Then Billy said, "I'm turning on a light. Don't look down."

The light on the wall was dim. The wall was made of rock and they had apparently just left the greenhouse behind them and entered a rough passageway. Kate looked back and saw that the corridor opened out from a wider, heavily leafed plantation of grape vines.

And she looked down at her feet too. Naturally.

The floor was alive with squirming piles of dark brown insects each about the size of her little toe. The insects, in fact, *were* the floor she was walking on.

Kate gasped. Billy said, "I told you not to look down. Don't worry – they won't hurt you and you can't hurt them. They're too well armoured. Nothing kills a cockroach. Do you know, a roach can live for days with its head cut off? Until it starves to death because it can't feed."

They were still moving onwards on the living carpet, crunching over it at a faster speed. Had they slowed, Kate would have fainted, but Billy propelled her forward as much by will-power as physical strength. Eventually she found the breath to say, "But there's millions of them! We never had them in the house…"

Billy glanced at her as they passed another of the lights on the wall. "They know their place. They're where they want to be and that's round here."

They were going down a slight incline all the time and Kate had the foreboding that they were travelling to something both unpleasant and very important. Billy said, "Hang on to me and close your eyes."

She obeyed, glad to be blind in a place like this. They came to a stop and light pinkened the darkness behind her squeezed-shut eyelids. Billy's voice was soft in her ear, "There is beauty too. Wonderful things. Open your eyes now."

There were a lot of lights here, in this chamber. Passages ran from it in all directions and yet it was not just a simple junction. Everywhere you looked were the carvings. They were the friezes on the walls and they were the pillars that separated the routes leading out of here. And what they depicted was a variety of life forms each of which had either human or insect characteristics or a mixture of the two. One pillar was an upright cockroach, wings and legs tucked in, whose delicate antennae were the supports for the roof. Another was a human leg, bent in the act of bearing weight. The pillars were most likely to be in the complex, serrated shape of an insect limb or feeler; while the friezes tended to show sad human faces staring out from patterns that were clearly based on the complex lens sets of insects' eyes. Some of these eyes were formed of close-packed globules, like caviar; others resembled … yes … that porous mesh… They looked like rounded teabags.

In the middle of the chamber, rising out of the little living roaches that crawled everywhere, it seemed a naked man was wrestling with a six foot cockroach: they were both upright and it took a moment to understand that they were really embracing. The quality of the rock carving was superb.

"That is talent," Billy breathed with respect. "What do you think, Kate? Their predicament perfectly expressed. Not bad for a people whose preferred diet is putrefied fruit and wallpaper paste."

"These aren't people," Kate said with abhorrence, looking at a frieze in which six human arms protruded from the thorax of a winged insect. "You keep saying people."

"Why not? They have the best attributes of people. Mutual respect, humility, sincerity … and they're the greatest builders who ever lived. They built your whole town in six months."

Kate was getting angry. The reaction came as a shock to her but she went with it. Maybe it was hysteria. "What else have you got to show me, then?"

"Plenty."

The passage he chose next had many others running off it in every direction. After taking three or four turnings, each of which led them on a steep upward incline, Kate understood she would never find her own way back. Higher up, the underfoot cockroaches petered out, and that was something. At the end of the low tunnel which the passageway had become, there was a top-storey view of another world.

The smoothly chiselled aperture was wide enough to accommodate them both. They were overlooking a cavernous arena from a hole that was replicated all around, so that it was like a subterranean coliseum, or even a cliff city from prehistory. There were four levels of these many entrances – or were they glassless windows? On the floor of the arena a well-attended ceremony was taking place, lit by four giant flaming braziers made of iron. The braziers were arranged in a square around a great raised oval of flecked bronze which was fixed in the rock floor and which seemed to be like a kind of altar to those assembled.

Kate recognized some of the faces as being those of passers-by on the streets, or customers she'd stood next to in the post office – but they were not human. They stood in well-delineated groups, each of which had a rigid cadaver held above their heads. The dead bodies were naked and grotesque in the extreme. Each had one or more insect deformities, most usually of the chest, back, or limbs. Each deformity was the colour of charcoal. One of the bodies had antennae trailing from its temples.

"They say farewell to their dead," Billy said. The mourners lifted their heads to look, and the "*Billy*" whisper went round. How many of them were there? Sixty? Must be.

"You see," Billy said more quietly. "See what your Jake has done?"

"No. He wouldn't kill anything."

"He fed them concrete powder and bit by bit they stopped moving. Right from the start there were digestive system problems. Too much acid. Simplifying the human process of waste elimination isn't easy."

Kate couldn't take that in. Her mind was operating on a more personal level. "I can't see your mother down there."

"You wouldn't. She's an ordinary person. Yes – *ordinary*," Billy said with loathing. "And weak. Just a follower."

"A follower of who?"

"Ortho. The great creator." There was less hatred in Billy's voice this time. He seemed to have mixed feelings about this Ortho. "He took his name from 'orthoptera' – the genus of roaches. And that's his little joke – to be known as Mr Roche down here."

"The *postman?*"

"You've seen how they love him. Especially the ridiculous 'Mr and Mrs Barton'. They worship him, because he chose them to play the parts of your neighbours. They think it means they're superior somehow."

Down by the braziers a group of these human-dressed mutants brought their dead friend or relation to the bronze centrepiece and laid him on it. Then each took off an article of clothing to reveal their own particular deformity. As they did so there came a chorus from the congregation. It went, "AHH!" Soft and sentimental, it was probably an expression of sympathy but it sounded more like the indulgent response of an elderly audience to an infant dancer.

"AHH!" they went again.

"They don't say much, do they," Kate remarked as a fact.

"Should have been there when they were learning their dialogue. The trouble we had with that…"

"So you're not one of them?"

"Know what I'd have liked to have been, Kate?"

"No."

"A footballer. I know I'm good enough. But it's not going to happen. Can't. Ever. Excuse me, but that guy was a friend."

These openings in the rock walls were indeed doorways. Chipped into the walls there were thousands of niches for foot and hand holds. Kate was startled to see how quickly Billy could scrabble down the perpendicular cliff face.

He walked to the focal point of the chamber and took off the track suit top Kate had never seen him without. Took off his T-shirt. Looked up at Kate defiantly.

Turned.

"AHH!"

Ichimura, conscious, was small and light. Semi-conscious, he put on a lot of weight after you had hauled him along for a kilometre or so. Fortunately he had been more active as they made the laborious climb out of the gully. Jake's fingers had turned into frozen claws in the effort to keep Icky upright and his immediate objective was to get to Blackhope Tower and find the medicine kit there. In some respects the worst time had been lying in the cold water waiting for their pursuers to surmount the intervening obstacles and find them still alive. That had not happened – either the paramilitaries believed no one could have survived the flaming fall or they had more pressing matters to attend to.

"Walk, will you? Move your legs up and down a bit!"

The mobile phone was broken. Jake had taken nothing from the panniers, not even the Ordnance Survey map, having a distrust of his ability to make use of it. However, the dyslexic sometimes has a wonderful, intuitive grasp of the big picture although he can't begin to sequence finer details, and all at once a warm spark of hope came to him. That heavier part of the night up ahead wasn't becoming a tree or a bush as they staggered nearer – it was a block that was something really big...

It was the tower.

He dragged Icky on with renewed strength, groundless optimism charging through him. Sure, try to fix Icky up, then go on to the castle just like they'd planned. It was all still possible.

"Walk! We're there! We're *there*!"

Even now he had to haul Ichimura round the tower as he looked for the door.

Ah. At last. There it was.

And it opened.

And Uncle Jimmy came out holding a hunting rifle. There were two men behind him, wearing their hair long, as he did.

The oh-so familiar voice said, in the oh-so friendly way, "Jake. Thought we'd gone our separate ways. Pleased to see me? Of course you are. I'm your Uncle Jimmy."

Jake's mind locked up and released itself in a split second. "I'm only here because you're in trouble. Big trouble."

"No, son, you're the one in trouble."

13

Billy's backbone had appeared quite normal, its bumps showing through the pale skin and making him appear vulnerable in the usual way. It was on either side of it that the mutant strains in him displayed themselves. There were two long narrow flaps like gills, that quivered and opened spasmodically, allowing access out of his body to the darker tissues, which corresponded to another fish-like attribute: fins. Only, they weren't fins, Kate knew, but another non-human extrusion. Billy's body had tried to develop wings. As a professional footballer, he would have had to steer well clear of the communal baths and showers.

She wanted to run but could not face the honey-comb maze of cockroach-infested passageways and tunnels. So she stayed in her window and waited for Billy to scamper back up the wall to her.

First there was the burial ceremony to complete. After the "Ahhing" was over there was a last prayer before the body was taken sorrowfully from the bronze artefact and carried off down one of the passages for disposal or interment.

The prayer was one word, said with deep feeling. Without any signal being given, the congregation said as one, softly, "Lovely." They all waited and you could sense them timing it and then they said again, "*Lovely*."

Billy put his clothes on and came back up the wall faster than a spider and Kate shrank back. He stayed crouched in the opening. She couldn't see his face clearly because the light was behind him.

He said, "You had to know. I wouldn't ever lie to you, Kate."

Kate tried to keep her voice steady. "You already have. Day after day after day."

"I want to help you. I want to look after you."

"Why?"

"Because you're beautiful. Because you're you."

"How could you look after me?" She couldn't hide the revulsion she felt.

"I'm rich. You don't know. There'd be a way. It's all I want – just to be together." He crept closer. "I'd never touch you. I'd never do anything you didn't want me to do."

She had to get out of here. In the confined space she wriggled past him so it was now she who overlooked the ceremonies chamber. Looking down at the grooves in the wall she thought she could just about make it if she had to. If Billy's grotesque friends let her...

Jake was sitting at the great table with the members of the Society for the Continuance of Mankind.

"He's only trying to make things better for himself," Jimmy remarked, in a brief lull in the questioning. "There's no military-style force coming here. What do you think, Stevie?"

The man whose day job was town disc jockey shrugged. "We've had phone calls about cars racing around the countryside – but nothing in our immediate vicinity. Some rowdy lot from the hotel? Your guess is as good as mine."

Billy Smith's mother, Lavinia, put a maternal point of view. "I'm very worried about Mr Kankuro."

"Junior or senior?" Ortho remarked in a sprightly way. He was fully-dressed and in such a neat fashion that it seemed he never slept at all.

"The young one."

"It's the older version that gives me cause for concern." Ortho gave the runaway all the power of a direct, hawk-like stare and Jake wondered how he'd ever swallowed the idea of this lordly old man being a small-town relief postman. "Neither you nor

Kankuro were in touch with anyone in the hours you were together?"

"I told you – there wasn't time."

"It's the first thing I would have done. And whatever your mutual failings might be, you're no fools, either of you."

"Listen. Ask yourself – where's Dr Dunning right now? I mean, thingy – Seton what's his name."

"Seton-Lindsay? Good point, Jake."

The Scot who was so much larger than Uncle Jimmy said in his light voice, "If he's not going to tell us anything useful we should get on and silence this young man."

Still toting the rifle, Uncle Jimmy said, at his least avuncular, "Break his neck and take him down South where he came from. Missing person found dead. Pure logic, end of story."

And end of Jake. Several animated voices made themselves heard to approve the plan or to denounce it as unthinkable.

"Well, let's ask the expert," Ortho overrode them. "Ralph – what's your take on this?"

Jake swivelled in his high-backed chair.

Ralph Seton-Lindsay was right behind him, holding a large leather pilot's bag. His cold eyes returned Jake's stare of astonishment without a flicker.

Ortho said to Jake with a twinkle, "Ralph got back an hour ago, having accomplished what he had left us to do. Nice try, young Jake, but no cigar."

175

Jake looked around wildly. Now they were never going to believe him. A spot of pink dotted his peripheral vision up on the gallery. Sholto. Eavesdropping and no doubt in a state of profound trepidation. Should he drag the gun-mad lunatic into this? Or hope that he might prove a friend in need if he was kept out of it?

"Ralph," Ortho prompted politely.

"All's well," the doctor said crisply. "I've done what I can for him and Mr Kankuro is sleeping now. With that gentleman a short but intensive course of suggestion and chemical reinforcements will obliterate the last weeks from his life. It's not even as if we have to replace his memories, so I have no doubts with him."

Jake blurted out, "But he was shot! And that's proof too, isn't it? That something's going on?"

Seton-Lindsay spoke to Ortho. "It looked to me as if a shard of metal had penetrated his side, most probably when the motorcycle fell. I looked most carefully for evidence of a gunshot wound – there was none."

Ortho gazed at Jake with helpless compassion. "And this boy? What of him?"

"He's already broken free of the control mechanisms once, against all the odds. I can make no guarantee with him. Take that as you will. Now, if you don't mind, I think we're forgetting the normal cycle of the Street. We don't want to lose the rest of

Team One through lack of attention to detail and I have a rainfall to arrange."

Without another word he strode off towards the exit under the stairs, where the castle continued in its many ramifications.

Jake thought palely, *He's sentenced me to death*.

There was silence around the long table. Maybe everyone else was considering Seton-Lindsay's words too. His mind went back to the happy times in the little house, with Stuart and Oona, and Kate… Much better never to have questioned anything, much better to have lived the lie and believed in it. Then he too could be warm in bed listening to the rain.

Rain? When it was an artificial world down there?

He took them by surprise when he jumped to his feet and ran at Seton-Lindsay at the door. At the last minute the man turned, alerted by the vibrations running through the floor from Jake's flying feet and the next second their bodies collided violently as Jake drove into his chest. The doctor's head snapped back and hit the door and he slid down it, dazed. Uncle Jimmy got to Jake shouting, "One more move and you're dead, sonny!" Jake took hold of the pilot's bag and swung it at the Scot, who jumped back.

Seton-Lindsay moaned, "Careful with the *bag*!"

Jimmy had the gun pointed now and Jake held the big pilot's case as a shield.

Seton–Lindsay shrieked at the top of his voice, "Not the *bag*!"

"Rain. The sprinkler system makes the rain. What's in the bag?" Jake asked breathlessly. "Why does he need the bag?"

The members of SCOM had left their seats. They stood aside as Ortho passed through them. He looked down at Seton–Lindsay and said conversationally, "Open the bag, Ralph."

The doctor worked his way to a standing position, sagging against the door. "Ortho. Don't be foolish. Obviously there's a lot to think about and I have important papers to go over in my room."

"Jolly good, Ralph," Ortho said appreciatively. "Open the bag."

"I didn't want them damaged. Obviously."

"I'm going to ask Jimmy to shoot you. And he will. Open the bag."

Seton–Lindsay took the case from Jake, who stood back, taking pleasure in the look of hatred he was given. It was the only time the doctor had ever shown any emotion at all. His hands were shaking as he worked the combination lock.

Ortho cast a quizzical eye on Jake. "The rain, yes… We had to use it one night when the sky opened by mistake… Was that what made you first suspect that all was not well with your surroundings?"

There was no time to answer that even if he had wanted to because at that moment the final tumbler on the lock clicked into place. Ortho at once stepped forward to take the bag from Seton-Lindsay's unresisting grasp. Snapped the top open. Drew out a large silver canister, on which there was the fine print of the manufacturer and, possibly, a sell-by date.

Ortho read from the canister and an icy fury rose in him. "Ralph. You have enough concentrated liquid insecticide here to crop-spray the whole of Scotland. I've a mind to make you drink it. You would have killed every living creature down there."

Stevie Morrison said slowly, "The boy was right, then? There's people coming?"

Ortho weighed up the information at his disposal. "Yes. And – one would guess – soon. Our chemical psychologist has rather cleverly turned himself into a Trojan horse. But we can be thankful at least that he's no longer available to open the front door to his friends."

A babble of consternation rose up. Ortho let it grow because, ever the gentleman, he felt it was required to give Jake a quiet, if neutral, nod of appreciation. Then he turned to his Society and his voice rang out over all the pandemonium. "Be silent!"

When the noise died down he continued in clear authoritative tones, "We have right on our side and we have trained for this kind of eventuality. We will not falter now!"

* * *

Kate was regretting her move to the lip of the upper-storey portal. She felt trapped between the mutants beneath and the would-be boyfriend so close behind her, at whom she still could not bring herself to look.

He was saying "Please" and she was saying "No", and they had explored almost every variation on that theme.

"Please look at me," he said now.

"No."

He tried another approach. "Turn round so I can see you and I'll tell you anything you want to know."

This was not such a bad bargain, she decided.

When she had turned herself round he said immediately, "You're so beautiful," and she re-estimated the worth of the deal. But it was done now.

The burial ceremony continued as they talked; solemn silences and "AHHs" and "*Lovelys*". Kate's first question was blunt and to the point. "How do I get out of here?"

"You can't. Not without me."

"Why am I here?"

He said, "I can save you – it's all right."

"Save me from what?"

"OK. OK." He was thinking about how best to explain it. "I'm … I'm an experiment. One that went wrong, but not as badly wrong as the others.

Honestly, Kate – I'm almost normal. I'm the best one they ever managed. By the time I was born they'd nearly got it right – I might even have a normal life-span. The others, well, they don't. The early ones are all dead – buried around here. They have rapid ageing problems. Average life-expectancy is about twenty years and at that age they look fifty. That hasn't happened to me – so you don't have to worry about that."

"All right. I won't."

"It's part of a plan to help the human race – to improve it. It's not anything evil. Ortho believes in life – not death – that's the whole point of every-thing we do. That's why he lets the people down here have their own lives … and their own children, so they can have as full a life as they can."

"Hang on. Ortho. Who's he?"

"He started all this. He's a scientist and … an entomologist … and … he's my father. I told you I was rich. I can get so much money – if we need it – I've been thinking about it and there'd be ways we could live a fabulous life."

"Stop it. You're only talking about yourself – I asked you about me."

"Yeah. OK. Yes. What it is, Kate – you're here to breed."

"Breed," she said flatly, fighting a worm of horror that swelled within her.

"Well – not *here* … in the world outside. The idea

was you wouldn't know you're any different to anyone else. He's going to breed certain strains into the population at large. By transgenesis."

"What have they done to me?" she asked, appalled.

"Oh – nothing. Not yet. You've only been prepared, so far. Then they … the new technique is to inject a culture into the womb shortly before the carrier of the genes reaches full maturity. There are so many problems to overcome. For instance, you've got to identify the right sub-species of roach. Can you imagine how hard that is?"

Kate couldn't and didn't want to. Lost in enthusiasm for his subject, Billy carried straight on. "Well, they went wrong for years by using *Blatella germanica*. I'm mostly *Periplaneta americana*, but the best guess now is that *Blatta orientalis* is the least hostile to the human immune system. It's only in the last three years he's finally found the trick of actually fine-tuning the master genes from the Oriental Cockroach."

"The trick? You call it a *trick*?"

"What does it matter now?" he said, surprised by her vehemence. "It's not going to happen to you. Not if you stick with me."

"You're mad, Billy. You must have inherited it from your father."

"I'm only trying to look after you. I need you, Kate." He reached out and put his hand on hers, whispering, "You come from nowhere. You belong nowhere. We're the same."

"You said you wouldn't touch me."

"I need you." He caressed her fingers, one by one.

"You don't need me, you need help."

Then he was angry. "It's Jake. You think he's so terrific – don't you? That's only because you've been programmed to love each other. So that you'd be looked after and survive to do what you were meant to!"

"Forget Jake. The point is, I don't want to be with you. Not now, not tomorrow, not ever."

He withdrew his hand and said bitterly, "If I had a choice, I still wouldn't want to be human. Who'd want to be that selfish and that destructive? I'm the way I am because someone wanted to save the human race and, you know something? You're not worth saving. None of you."

Now he was sulking and she'd blown her chance to find out more. She felt sorry for him and at the same time he scared her.

His father was more terrifying still. When she saw him Kate had no doubt as to his identity. Trim and narrow, you could see the resemblance between him and Billy, when you knew.

The burial ceremony had been interrupted by murmurs of awe and astonishment. Kate and Billy went to look and the mourners had been joined by the Laird of Broomcleuch – and Mr and Mrs

Barton, who stood behind him very self-importantly. Mrs Barton held her shapeless knitting clutched to her chest like a badge of office.

Ortho raised his hand paternally, "Please, my children, do not be alarmed. You know I would not come amongst you in your private areas unless there was good reason. And may I say how magnificently you have constructed this – well – one would have to call it a temple, wouldn't one?" He beamed at his assembled creations, looking all around. And his gaze fixed on Kate and Billy in their eyrie.

"Beautiful," he smiled radiantly. "Beautiful,"

It was the most sinister thing she had ever heard. She spun round, barged past Billy and broke into a crouching run.

Billy shouted, "Wait, Kate – don't!"

To lose him she took the first turning she came upon and, after that, the second.

And of course succeeded in losing herself completely.

14

The idea of torturing Ralph-Seton Lindsay for information had been discussed and rejected on moral grounds. He was now locked in a meat safe off the kitchen area with Jake as his companion. The meat safe was in fact a small cold room with thick, if crumbling, walls and the only meat in it was its two human occupants.

Tense and angry, Seton-Lindsay was uncharacteristically voluble and Jake had already learned that Billy was Sir William Carrick-Boyd's mutant son. Seton-Lindsay was more interested in speaking about the father, however.

"He's barking mad. The whole family is. What is the point of delaying the inevitable? It's over."

"Yes," Jake agreed, to keep him talking. "What is?"

Seton-Lindsay thought for a while and smiled. It was an unfriendly expression that made its way to his face. "Pass the time, shall we? It'll be like a séance – talking to a dead person."

"Why – what d'you mean?"

"The men who are coming here are going to get in and do what they were sent to do. Which is – since you were about to ask – to search and destroy. Lift the science and torch the rest. Which includes you and every member of that absurd secret society."

"So where do you fit in?" Jake asked with assumed nonchalance.

"When the Berlin Wall came down, there were a lot of covert operatives laid off. My own skills, in chemically oriented interrogation techniques, were considered redundant. Then Ortho approached me, offering money he'd raised from certain multi-national companies. I was happy to help because of the possibilites I saw."

"I don't think anyone's going to have to kill me because of what I know," Jake said. "Because I didn't understand a word of that."

"Well let's do it Jackanory, then," Seton-Lindsay said contemptuously. "Ortho is nothing but an ageing hippie who's obsessed by the idea of a nuclear meltdown. Gets himself some flower power followers in the nineteen-sixties and sets up as a saviour of the universe. They're a dedicated bunch – I'll give them that. Young men and women who were prepared to make babies … of a certain kind. A kind that would withstand nuclear fallout. And there, if you come from my background, is the Armageddon scenario we worked so long and so hard to avoid. Ortho won't see it, but once you create a version of *Homo sapiens* that can survive a radiation holocaust, why, then you can go ahead and have your nuclear war just like you always wanted to. It's the nature of science and the true meaning of progress. You do something not because it's right or wrong, *but because it can be done*. Which is why I've suggested continuing this research with mantid genes. Get a bit of aggression into the new race. In any war, one will still need soldiers…"

"And that's what you want?" Jake said, dumb-founded. "Total mayhem?"

"When you work in the field I do, it's extremely hard to retain any respect at all for the individual man or woman," Seton–Lindsay mused. "What is the human race, anyway? A collection of organisms who live for a little while and then die, one way or another. So what's the difference? What I mean, Jake, is – what do people *matter*?"

It was at this point that Billy was thrown into the room, rather gently, by two late-middle-aged members of SCOM. They left, re-locking the door.

"Ah, Billy," Seton–Lindsay said. "Out of favour? Or here to prise from me my darkest thoughts?"

Billy gave Jake a cold dark look before he answered the chemical psychologist.

"You think I'm out of favour, you should hear what they're saying about you."

"And from such gentle people too," Seton-Lindsay remarked with mock surprise.

Then Billy said to Jake, "You're the lowest thing that ever lived. You poison Kate against me and you poison my people."

"I didn't. I didn't do either of those things."

"My father says I can't be trusted any more. What about you – pouring concrete into the food mix?"

"Ah – no, no," Seton-Lindsay interrupted affably, "that was me. It seemed advisable to slow a few of your friends down, Billy, given the sheer weight of their numbers in time of conflict. Your erstwhile chum here has, in fact, saved them all from painful extinction since then. Just wanted to put the record straight."

"Really?"

"Where's Kate?" Jake asked Billy, who went on staring at Seton-Lindsay very deliberately. It was like he was taking a mental snapshot of him with some kind of advanced photo system that would stamp the picture, "*Rubbish – dispose of carefully*".

"Kate, yes…" he answered Jake distantly. "I've gone off her."

"But where is she?"

Billy was thinking about something else altogether

and, as a consequence, the lie was so casually delivered that it was believable. "Um ... I'm not sure. We were together ... and then we got split up."

Kate had no idea where she was either. She couldn't open her eyes, nor remember the last half-hour of her life. Not yet. She was in a small dark universe of semi-consciousness, faintly aware that something very important was taking place, or had taken place. As her mental capacities reasserted themselves, sudden sharp images erupted into her brain. The flight in the tunnels; the ghastly roach-people who dwelt deeper in, more insect than man... And with the images came the aural memory of the gentle "AHH" of Billy's people. Which directed her mind to the burial ceremony.

The ritual she recalled was grander by far than it had been at the time, accompanied as it was now by inspirational choral music of a heavily religious nature.

Kate had never before heard the Vivaldi *Gloria*, so stirring, so uplifting, so ... glorious.

"*Gloria in excelsis Deo*," the choir sang, bursting with majesty, and Kate opened her eyes and the music was louder and more brilliant as she returned to the real world – the real world which, here, was entirely fabricated of cinema screens.

She was strapped tightly into some sort of dentist's chair in a large octagonal space whose walls were projection panels, each showing a nuclear explosion. Colour film alternated with black and white footage of notable atomic test explosions – the mushroom clouds rising in layers like wedding cakes – the astonishing brilliance of the actual explosion – the waves of destructive energy reaching out like Saturn's rings with a steady and remorseless grandeur – and all set to Vivaldi's sublime music of praise.

How had she ended up in this bizarre place? Oh yes. Finally, she had run straight into Mr and Mrs Barton. They hadn't said much, but they had been pleased to see her...

"You're awake!" came a high cry. Directly behind her – and she couldn't turn to see him – was Ortho, who was forced to shout at the top of his voice to surmount his audio-visual presentation of the destructive power of the great Bomb.

He came round to stand in front of her, trim and grandfatherly, smiling broadly. In a moment of random bathos, she realized he had false teeth.

"The end of the world, Kate!" he bawled with dancing eyes and with that manic grin stretching even wider. "But you're going to do something about it!"

There was a lot of hustle and bustle in the castle by the sound of it. Hunched in a corner, Seton-Lindsay was listening intently for any stray noise that might announce a change in their circumstances, while at the same time his nerves made him garrulous in a superior sort of way.

"No blame attaches to me, Billy. Your father started his own downfall when he got into bed with big business. It's no way to keep a secret, is it?" He directed his attention to Jake. "You see, there are beneficial side-effects as a result of this extraordinary process. Did you know that genetic defects can cause leukaemia before birth? Well, not if you're one of Ortho's brood. The pharmaceutical companies got highly-edited information, enough to make them throw money his way, and at the same time he exploited the simple passivity of his new beings, who have such enormous skill with their hands. Imagine a factory workforce that works hard and never considers taking industrial action! What a tempting carrot that was! I tell you, if it hadn't been me who let the cat out of the bag, it would have been someone else with even worse intentions."

"How could anyone have worse intentions than you?" Billy commented coolly.

Seton-Lindsay did not respond at first. All three prisoners were listening to a new sound. A scraping, scratching noise coming from under their feet.

Billy queried brightly, "Your lot? Or mine…"

"Doesn't matter – there's only going to be one outcome here." But Seton Lindsay was patently uneasy. As they listened they went on with their conversation automatically.

"If you want to know the real monstrosity in all this," Billy said, "it's you."

"Oh no – your father is the monster here and you might as well believe it. He was the prime mover in everything! It was not *my* idea to sweep up all those unfortunates from the streets. They may not have had much, but they had their freedom. You've enjoyed your little period of independence, haven't you, Jake?"

"How many of us have you kidnapped?" Jake demanded to know.

Listening hard as he did so, Billy answered that. "There's another team waiting to move into your house when you leave. And two more in their earliest days. They've each got their own Uncle Jimmy, but he's the original and the best. Son of my father's estate manager." He flicked a glance at Seton-Lindsay, "Loyal as they come."

The room shook a fraction of a second before they heard the deep thud of the explosion. Seton-Lindsay got to his feet. "Classic! The attack just before dawn! The beginning of the end, Billy!"

Billy said evenly, "You're not worth killing, Ralph, because you're hardly alive in the first place," and Seton-Lindsay laughed – and at one and the same time the door crashed in and one of the slabs that made the floor lifted up as if it was weightless.

At the door, whose great iron hinges had almost broken off, there stood a factory worker in the overalls that covered his less human attributes. His face broke into a smile at seeing Billy. "Ooh – lovely!"

Jake was looking at the hole in the floor. The thing that was coming up through it could never be taken for human under any circumstances. It had a broadly ribbed thorax and a metallic back-plate and four crooked charcoal-coloured limbs that ended in the shape of pliers. Poking out between its bug-like stomach and a cowl formed by the top of its back-plate was the grey pulpy triangle that was its face, with deep eyeholes visible immediately beneath two drooping antennae. Its mouth came into focus when four wet feelers appeared at the very bottom of its visage and it delivered itself of its entire vocabulary in one sloshing, hissing, inevitable word.

"*Lovely!*" it said.

Seton-Lindsay was pressed back against the wall in terror. Billy smiled at him. "Might see you later, then. Got to rush." To Jake he said, "See – my father may be King, but I'm the Crown Prince!" and to his faithful bugmen, "Things to do – this way!"

He ran and dived head first down the hole and his followers … followed.

Jake went too – the other way, out through the door. Lord knows where Billy was headed but he was going to find Kate. He heard gunfire from above. If the walls had been breached and the invading force was attempting entry it might be too dangerous to try and get to the main lift…

Trapped in the chair, Kate pulled on the restraining bands, which were made of nylon-like suitcase straps. The result was a nasty friction burn. The choir sang and on the walls the bombs went off all around her. They had felt the vibrations from the real explosion in the castle and Ortho had only grinned at her again and gone behind her to go on with whatever it was he was doing there.

Now he came back into view, humming along to the music. "Not long now!" he shouted encouragingly. "The culture has to be at precisely the right temperature and I can't heat it too quickly. It's not something you can microwave!"

She had to do something. She couldn't just sit here and wait to become a mother of insect hybrids. Ignoring the pain, she spread her fingers wide and stretched every tendon in her wrists, making her hands look as big as possible. "It hurts," she whimpered with a realism that was not all feigned.

"What?" Ortho couldn't hear her and appeared oblivious, too, to the discharges of gunfire coming from the Great Hall.

"I can't feel my fingers," she said more loudly. He disappeared from sight and the music cut out. The shooting beyond the locked door was sharp and clear in their ears – the rattle of automatic fire, the crack of rifle-shooting and the deeper percussive notes of shotguns. Back in front of her he said impatiently, "What. What is it?"

"My hands… I can't feel them."

His expression read, "This is an irritatingly minor detail at a time like this," but he was a gentleman and unversed in prisoner-captor relations, so he tut-tutted at the state of her wrists and loosened the straps a little.

He stayed right by her, so close that she felt his breath caress her face. The glare from the lights in the ceiling created a shining halo around his white hair. He said raptly, "A simple injection and we can move on from here. You will breed, Kate, and the world will be safe. No one can imagine the horror of nuclear devastation – its enormity is beyond comprehension and when a vision of it creeps into our mind's eye we look away, unwilling to acknowledge the possibility of something so disturbing. But just think – a power station accident – an act of terrorism… This terrible technology is available almost across the counter! But with your involuntary help there will be a people who can survive the day of reckoning, and they will be humble and gentle, a people that can be led. You see, Kate, as my researches progressed, I found much to encourage me in my work. Signs, you might say, from Above. We are a species out of control, destroying our own planet; unappealing and ungovernable! But after your reproductive system has been inextricably linked to a magnificent species that is three million years old and has the capacity to survive almost everything, including Man and his vile nuclear devices, my modified race shall spread and prosper in loving harmony and it shall be pleasing to His eye."

His own eye went from hers to glance at his watch. "Aha!" he said and went away.

The gunfire abated. Kate worked at the straps. There was now just a chance she could extricate herself from them, but it would take some work.

Then Ortho was back at her side, bearing a hypodermic syringe. It was a large instrument built wholly of steel, as if glass were not strong enough to contain whatever was in it. The needle was of steel too.

Her face must have registered the terror she felt. He stroked her cheek with his free hand. "Be calm. This is a time for rejoicing."

There was a loud bang and the door to the hall flew open, its mighty lock shattered. Against all logic, Kate prayed it was Jake, come to get her.

It wasn't.

15

Jake's helter-skelter progress down the spiral stairway he had seen with Sholto brought him to a secret entrance to the surgery in the Street. The underground building was much larger than he had ever thought and in finding his way out he found Ichimura Kankuro.

Icky was lying tied to a workbench in a large room leading off Seton-Lindsay's consulting room. It looked like a dirty old engineering works, crammed with lathes and basins and cisterns and with lengths of metal and plastic piping lying around. A perfect place to learn plumbing, in fact...

"Hey!" Icky said faintly on seeing him.

"Yeah – hey. How you doing?"

"Oh, pretty fine. The doctor guy fixed me up good. What gives?"

"We've got to get out of here." Jake was already unbuckling him from the chair.

"OK – tell me later."

Getting out of the chair the bandaged Icky winced, said "Oof," and fell over.

Jake said, "I thought you said you were fine."

"Well, everyfing's comparative."

Back in the business of supporting Icky, Jake took them out through the exit he knew, through the empty waiting room and out on to the familiar street in its night-time state, with street-lamps lit.

Across the road the flour factory sighed deep in its foundations and collapsed, coming straight towards them in a tidal wave of bricks. At the same time the sky fell in.

The visitors to Ortho's laboratory were Ralph Seton-Linsdsay and two muscular men wearing black track-suits and balaclavas and carrying machine-pistols. Seton-Lindsay had a shotgun, taken from one of the castle's defenders.

He was not openly triumphant. "You really are a stubborn man, aren't you, Sir William? You'll notice I don't call you Ortho. That was finished the moment the boy broke loose from us. Did you really think the family unit could survive his defection? I had to bring forward my own plans very quickly after that. And in pursuit of those plans I now require your keys."

"You can't have them," Ortho said with dignity. He held on to the hypodermic tightly, too, Kate observed.

"I don't need them, you understand. I know where everything is – it's just a matter of getting what we want without making too much of a mess."

It was a little late for that, for it was at this minute that the foundations of Broomcleuch, already weakened by much excavation, gave way in the vicinity of the flour factory below the front entrance of the castle, causing most of the glass floor of the hall to cascade down into the street it overlooked. In here the eight cinema screens went blank.

After the initial shock Seton–Lindsay quickly transferred his gaze back to Ortho, a predator keen that his prey should not escape. He said to the paramilitaries, "Check it out."

Kate worked on the straps. The joints on the base of her thumbs were the sticking point and one of her wrists was already bleeding.

One of the men reported, "Floor's gone. Everything else holding steady. Major casualties." He had a foreign accent Kate couldn't place. Clouds of brick dust wafted through the doorway. The men again took up their places at either side of and just behind Seton–Lindsay.

"You … *destroyer*," Ortho spluttered at him.

"I need those keys. Now. Time's running out."

Ortho began to prevaricate and Kate could see why. Two portly human shapes were emerging through the dust cloud at the door and one of them held her precious knitting.

Mr and Mrs Barton.

"I think there's something you ought to know," Ortho said to Seton-Lindsay, making it up as he went along, "The culture container ... it's, um, wired to explode if anyone tampers with it."

"It's not. Now give me the keys." Seton-Lindsay took a few steps forward and raised the shotgun. "I'll count to three and then I'll just come and get them myself. You'll be dead, so you won't mind."

One of Kate's hands came free with a jerk. No one noticed.

Seton-Lindsay said clearly, "One."

Mrs Barton had extracted her knitting needles from the woollen muddle of the moment and handed one to her husband. Expressionless, they quietly stepped forward.

Kate's attention went to the strap that held her other hand and she missed the moment when the needles found their targets. Looking up briefly she saw the Bartons moving forward and two tracksuited bodies on the floor. However, Ortho's silence and fixed expression was the undoing of his would-be rescuers. Kate got the buckle free at the exact moment Seton-Lindsay whirled round and fired the shotgun twice, emptying it of both cartridges. When Kate leaned forward to work on the single strap that held her feet, an appalling sight met her eyes.

The Bartons no longer had heads and they were still moving towards Seton-Lindsay, their last living intention driving them on inexorably. There wasn't much blood to be seen and where it glistened on their shattered necks it was as dark as black treacle. Without a thought in their minds, without minds at all, they were going to accomplish what they had set out to do.

Panicking, Seton-Lindsay turned to Ortho, who was watching the drama unfold with more sorrow than relish.

"Ortho – stop them!"

"How?" Ortho asked simply.

Kate tugged at the buckle.

What was left of Mr and Mrs Barton reached Seton-Lindsay.

The deafening onrush of bricks and masonry had missed Jake and Icky by a whisper as they fell back into the doorway of the surgery. The noise of breaking glass was everywhere. They lay where they had fallen for many moments, coughing in the dust that had been thrown up.

Jake pulled Icky back up on to his feet and tugged him along in the search for Kate. Driven by the force of his need to find her, they surmounted the pile of rubble and staggered over bricks and glass to get to the Higgins' house. Lying here and there, hugging the asphalt, were other obstacles – the bodies of those fallen from the hall. Members of SCOM, grey-haired, in company with a dozen or so men in black sports gear. Men who had not so very long ago booked into the Cheviot Peregrine Hotel as physio-therapists. There were no factory workers to be seen and no policemen, and no one from Taylor's. And no Kate – but outside the house he had believed was his home Jake saw Stuart and Oona. Stuart was pulling at his wife, directing her to get into the Bartons' three-wheeler car.

Well, they wouldn't get very far in *that*.

In arguing the point with them – they were all shouting at the top of their voices – he pointed up at the sky, which no longer existed. In its place was a jagged hole and a view of, from what seemed hundreds of metres up, the painted ceiling of the Great Hall.

"There's nothing there! It just stops!" he bellowed. Looking around wildly for other proof that they were in a world no more real than a cardboard toy theatre, he saw that up at the end of the street the gate in the spear-tipped fence around the pylon swung open. Raising his gaze, he was rewarded by the sight of Mr and Mrs Barton, miniature at this distance, climbing up the far side of the pylon – right up into the castle. The pylon, it appeared, was also an emergency exit.

The reason for his being here came back with a rush. "Where's Kate?" he shrieked.

"Gone, son!" Oona bawled back in great distress.

"We can't find her anywhere!" Stuart chipped in hoarsely. "It's all my fault – I was feeling so funny! Not like myself at all!"

It seemed to Jake that the only other place she was likely to be was up in the castle. Behind them, the surgery cracked its walls and suddenly sat itself down a few metres below the level of the street, and it was obvious that the only way to get to her was to follow their mountaineering neighbours up the pylon.

"Stick with me," he shouted, and dragged Icky on up the street, into which there still fell stray shards of shattering glass. As they hurried past Taylor's, where the glasshouses lay in ruins, they saw creepers and passageways and carvings reaching back into the soft rock and two workers with pickaxes who were pounding into one of the supporting pillars of stone…

"You!" Stuart stopped to confront them. "What do you think you're up to? Save yourselves!"

Jake commanded, "Get on – leave them!"

One of the overalled labourers smiled mildly at Stuart and cleared his throat of the omnipresent dust. He called out politely, "Debuilding. We unbuilding."

The other was helpful too, explaining, "Billy *said* to."

Jake got it instantly. "He's going to bring the whole place down – now move yourselves!" he yelled.

Kate got to the back door of the laboratory only a second or two before Ortho. In dashing to it her legs had gone rubbery and she had fallen against one of the workbenches. They were in her way everywhere – tables made of aluminium, laden with a diversity of beakers, retorts and machines, some of which resembled expensive chrome–plated percolators or toasters. To herself, she seemed to be moving in slow motion to a soundtrack of toppling scientific instruments.

The door did not budge, pull on it as she might. Ortho's hand came over her shoulder and pressed against it just in case she might have been able to tug it open. He had very clean nails – it was a surgeon's hand.

He said, "If you're going anywhere, my dear, it will be with me. You're far too precious to lose."

Something tickled by the side of her jaw. He had the hypodermic just touching the skin there.

"I think you should do just what I say. I couldn't answer for the outcome if the contents of this found their way into your neck."

One by one the street lamps were extinguished as power cables were severed.

The pylon's very presence in the street was explained by its dual function – it was a necessary support for the floor above as well as being an access point. Apart from a head for heights, no great climbing skills were needed, for concealed metal ladders ran up the struts at the back. The question was, would this mighty prop survive Billy's efforts to bring down the whole castle before they reached the top?

The labyrinth of tunnels and passages and filigree pillars under the foundations made the job of debuilding a lot less arduous than it might have been.

On their way up one of the steel ladders, Jake and Icky were lagging behind Stuart and Oona, who were ascending the second mighty brace across the way. The street was dark and dead. Reaching down to help Icky beneath him Jake could just make out the moment when the post office deconstructed itself noisily into a smoking heap of building materials. His own house and that of the Bartons went much more quickly, subsiding straight down into the ground as if a giant trapdoor had opened.

The recreation ground tilted. The police station as yet held firm, though the car park lower down was breaking up as a series of seismic ripples ran across its surface, leaving jagged lines in the tarmac. The driverless bus that was parked there made nervous movements back and forth.

They had a way to go yet and his arm felt as if it

would break unless he let go of Icky. He saw when, as if fatally undecided as to which way to run, the bus jammed itself in a larger split that had opened in the car park and was gradually swallowed down by the widening maw.

The structure they were climbing narrowed at the top like a regular pylon, then widened again, reaching out its arms of support to the floor above, which began where the glass roof, when it existed, had ended, near the far end of the hall. In normal circumstances the arc lights in the glass would have blinded anyone looking up at the top of the pylon, where a platform gave access to a trapdoor to the castle proper.

Stuart and Oona were scrambling up through the open trapdoor when the police station sagged and tumbled down, wall by wall. The pylon lurched and Jake and Icky were nearly thrown off. It began to lean perilously to one side and groaned and screeched and twanged, calling out terrible noises of metallic stress.

But it held. It held and Jake was able to haul Icky up to the platform and shove him up into the hall. A last glance down through the billowing dust-clouds showed him the fearful force of Nature at work. All along this strata in the local topography ran the massive fault in the land. It made the chasm he had found in front of the fake flats; it caused the ravines that he and Icky had tried to leap on the motorcycle.

And, encouraged by Billy Carrick-Boyd, it was greedy. It sent out fingers of destruction and pulled at the street itself and dragged it down.

The dust rose up, ever-increasing in volume, and what was left of the underground suburb that purported to be part of a town in the Midlands of England was hidden from view.

In the Great Hall itself there was structural unease. You felt it very ominously even though here the electric lights were all still working. Parental ties forgotten, Stuart and Oona were edging their way around the edge of the gorge that had once been the glass floor. Jake saw them skirting by a black, blood-stained rug that had once been Sholto's beloved Trajan. Farther on, the main entrance to the castle had been blown open and lying there with three others of his force was the leader of the physiotherapists, shot through the head.

Stuart and Oona stepped over them fastidiously and went out into the world, where a new dawn was breaking.

"Follow them," Jake choked, then grabbed Icky's arm. "No – wait."

Across from where they had arrived at the top of the trapdoor there were living human beings. They stood so very still Jake had not noticed them at first. A section of the wall under the minstrel's gallery had either been blown in or had fallen down, and it revealed the interior of one of the rooms under the picture gallery. It was a cosy room with a battered sofa and a glass-topped coffee table, and a big mirror over the coal-effect gas fire that had flickered so warmly on winter evenings...

The old house – with its new inhabitants, who stood loose-armed staring at nothing at all. A man, a woman, and a girl, in dressing gowns.

"How are you now?" Jake asked Icky.

His injured companion gasped out, "I fink I got a second wind. What now?"

"Get round to those people and lead them out. As quick as you can. I think you'll find they're pretty obedient."

"Why – what are you gonna do?"

"I've got to find my ... I've got to find Kate. You save them. They need help."

Pale and weak, Icky was still able to give him a stern stare. "You sure?"

"Sure."

"You got it."

Jake left him to it and went into the part of the castle he knew nothing of, starting with Ortho's laboratory, where several people lay dead and, intertwined among them, Seton-Lindsay and the Bartons, with a single head between them. Jake gave the gruesome sight no more than a cursory glance on his way to the end of the room, which led straight through to another large laboratory and thence to a broad hallway. The pictures on these walls were trembling. Sir William Carrick-Boyd's forebears were rightly concerned about the condition of the ancestral home.

"Kate?" Jake called. "KATE!"

Somehow it didn't seem too wise to shout, in case the least added vibration accelerated the castle's demise. A set of large double doors looked promising and he went through them.

It was an entrance into the castle chapel, behind the high altar. He couldn't help but draw in the serenity of the place as he walked down the aisle. The place of worship was quiet and old with narrow arched windows and with the tranquillity that comes from being built for something more than mortal purposes.

It had stood for generations but it wouldn't be here much longer. The stone-paved floor was being hit by small, searching tremors.

The main doors opened out under a sturdy arch on to the hillside at the back of the castle, where it was cold and fresh and the land rolled away in a gentle decline to the moors. As it can be, the dawn light was eerie and apocalyptic.

Kate and Ortho were only a few hundred metres away, walking down the hill in what appeared to be a friendly embrace. Jake could not know they were walking so slowly because the ground was uneven and Kate had a hypodermic pressed to her neck.

He started to run. Then heard the shouting and stopped. Looked back and up.

High on one of the four corner towers, their heads and torsos visible above the stone crenellations, were three of those who had lived in the Castle.

Sholto, in tweeds, with a rifle he wanted to use. Uncle Jimmy, shouting, trying to stop him. Billy's mother, screaming, in turn trying to stop Uncle Jimmy.

Jake could see Uncle Jimmy reaching for the rifle and batting it aside as Sholto raised it for a second time. He saw Billy's mother striking at Uncle Jimmy – a woman suddenly brought back to life and with a purpose – and clasp and then wrench him away from Sholto.

In one practised movement Sholto brought up his hunting rifle and aimed and fired in almost a single movement, with all the confidence of one who is good at only one thing and has twenty-twenty vision to aid him.

Jake spun round. Ortho had fallen. Kate and Jake were looking at each other, separated by distance and impending disaster.

Ortho gone, reduced to the status of a small, dead white-haired man, the castle was about to topple too, as if it had no reason now to go on holding itself up.

Dyslexia and intuitive design sense – instead of running down the hill, when Jake felt the immense tremor under his feet he belted back to the archway of the chapel doors instead, and thus avoided being pulped by falling ruins. Very strong shape, the arch.

From where she stood, far from danger herself, Kate saw him running back, retreating from her, and couldn't understand it. Then she saw the towers waver and crumble down, becoming shorter and shorter, and saw the castle walls billowing out.

The fine old building collapsed gracefully, outwards, quite slowly.

Light pierced through the gritty gloom from somewhere high up, making its way through a muddle of broken stonework that had settled itself any old how, one slab balanced precariously on another. The arch had held but it was a very small space Jake found himself in when he woke after having been knocked out by a glancing blow from a wooden beam.

Something was coming towards him. He heard it crawling and puffing out bubbling breaths as it approached through the fallen stones and bricks. Some cockroach creature, no doubt, well-nigh indestructible.

Painfully, it tried to worm its way through a small opening in the stones. It had a human head and it was Sholto. He was literally a broken man but his stupidity had not yet allowed him to recognize this. He recognized Jake, though.

"Orh. It's you." His muffled voice made a series of grunting noises. "Orh. I'm stuck. Never mind. Let me tell you, it was a long way down. Think I might have hurt myself."

"You shot Ortho," Jake told him, in case it had slipped his mind.

"Bill," Sholto corrected him. "My brother, Bill." He stopped trying to move and lay there with only his top half as company for Jake. "Yes, I shot Bill. Shot a lot of people. See – I put my hunting things on – good camouflage, d'you see. Up there on the gallery. Couldn't wear pink. Rather imagine it was me who saved the day."

"If you say so."

Sholto looked up at him with those blue, blue eyes. "You know, when I sent you out, I didn't mean for you to do all this," he said sternly, if weakly.

"It wasn't me. Things just kind of happened."

"Orh yes. Isn't that always the way. My word, I'm tired."

His voice was fading. Jake crawled a little closer.

"Why did you kill your brother?"

In the darkness Sholto said faintly, "I saw the light. It wasn't just he wanted my organs. He wasn't … behavin' properly. Horrible things, he made … and it was his fault they wrecked Broomcleuch. Our birthright. It just came to me, 'Shoot the swine'."

His eyes were closing. Under the mask of bruises, blood and brick dust he looked peaceful.

Then the blue eyes flickered into life again. "Nice to be with someone. It's dark down here. You know – did I tell you? – I always wondered what it would be like to shoot someone."

212

"Yes, you told me."

"It's … orh." He took a deep and desperately painful breath. "Orh. Awful. And Trajan's dead too. Never get another dog like him. Think I might give up huntin', when I'm better."

"Yes," Jake said quietly.

"You tired, too?" Sholto whispered. "I am. But I'll get by. Tough as boots, me. It's in the blood."

And he died.

Before Jake could worm his way back under the arch there was a sudden fall of rubble and he was crushed down into complete blackness. He was only half conscious when the helicopters came over the horizon and flew down, making an increasingly loud *chop-chopping* noise, as choppers should.

17

It wasn't so much a hospital as a clinic, Jake had decided. Certainly clinical, if the antiseptic smells were anything to go by. The nurses avoided conversation, their lips as stiff and starched as their uniforms. From them he learned only that he had suffered bad concussion and had fractured ribs. A high, complicated bed, white walls and a garishly yellow blind covering the windows at all times – this had been his environment for two days.

A poker-faced Japanese man brought him clothes. Smart clothes that Jake would never in a million years have chosen for himself: narrow shiny trousers and a deep blue turtleneck sweater to go over them. Waste of – probably – a lot of money.

The Japanese man said in perfect American

English, "I translate for Mr Kawatake Kankuro. You're going to meet with him. As we leave, or at any time, do not attempt to talk to anyone of your experiences. OK?"

"Why?"

"That's just the kind of thing we don't want. No questions, kid. You'll be told what you need to know. Until then, just button your mouth."

It was he who signed the paperwork at reception. Looking through the glass frontage Jake saw it was a gleaming wet night outside, with a lot of traffic sweeping by. They walked out into a big city street. Jake's walking wasn't too good. Maybe he'd been in bed for a while. Thankfully it was not far to the limousine.

When they went round Trafalgar Square Jake understood that he was in London, although he had never heard of the posh and sublimely discreet hotel that was their destination. A silent lift took them to the top floor, where Japanese men waited in well-tailored suits; men who, from their physiques, could have made excellent physiotherapists.

Mr Kankuro's suite must have taken up most of the floor. The lobby seemed bigger than the whole house they had lived in at Broomcleuch. Icky looked comically small, standing there in clothes much like Jake's. They shook hands.

"How you going, Jake? Like the sweater? I chose it myself."

"You're kidding," Jake said.

"Turns out you got hurt worse than I did. But you're OK now – yes?"

"Sure." And then he asked the only question that really mattered. "Where's Kate?"

"She's in good shape. Listen, I got my orders, Jake. There's stuff we got to go through."

He'd see her. She was safe… Was it because he was programmed to desire her safety that it mattered so much? Or was it something else, and if it wasn't something else, did it matter?

Because he was thinking that through, he only half-heard Icky's dissertation on his future, sitting in the lobby after the translator had left.

The gist of it was that he was going to be all right. Because Mr Kankuro had influence. Because he could fix things. The price for fixing things was silence. There would even be a contract to sign.

"You're going to be placed with KK employees – Brits. They never even heard of John Buchan – can you believe that – but they're not too bad and you'll only have to have a couple of years with them, being the age you are."

"Whatever. You got those people out, did you?"

"No problem. In the end they were the ones carrying me out."

"And Stuart and Oona – they're OK?"

"They're fine. Well, they got problems but… But you don't ask that. You don't see them ever again.

216

That all right with you?"

"Yes. We, er, we weren't close. Not really…"

"You knew them only a few months. True fact."

"Where did the helicopters come from?"

"Can't tell you. It was an arrangement. Top level. My dad was in Paris, see, and after your calls he…"

"He fixed things."

"He does have that knack."

"I'm feeling a bit tired…"

"Sure, sure. We'll go see my dad now. The paperwork can wait."

The drawing room of the suite was opulently furnished in pale pinks and blues and the furniture was gold-legged and, basically, impractical. One would have to guess that Kawatake Kankuro travelled in his own chair, for he was seated in a black leather electronically-operated recliner, with a glass of whisky at his elbow. He was a short, square man and at this moment he was wearing full evening dress with an air that suggested he was rarely out of it. He got up and bowed slightly to Jake, who found himself returning the bow with haste, as Westerners do at such times.

The smooth skin on Mr Kankuro's face was scored with deep lines around the mouth and eyes. His hair was as black as his eyes, which were fathomless and steady. He could have been any age between fifty and seventy.

Now he spoke in Japanese in a bronchial growl,

sounding intensely angry and waving a hand at the drinks table.

"My father says you must eat and drink. Do it – it'll make him happy."

Jake was learning the old lesson that the very rich expect to get their own way and very quickly.

He took a Coke and some cashews. "Thank you," he bowed to Mr Kankuro, who nodded back sharply before resuming his seat. He began to talk at a great rate, in the same imperious growl.

When he stopped, Icky translated. "My father says thank you for saving his son's life. That's me, and in my opinion I'd have managed OK without you but he's made up his own mind about that. He says you are resourceful, which is the highest praise, coming from him."

Jake nodded cautiously at Mr Kankuro and Mr Kankuro nodded back. And spoke again. Icky translated again. "In business there are many who seek to bring you down. Sometimes in maintaining the edge you are drawn into affairs that are not worthy of you. And sometimes you must get your hands dirty to learn what the competition may be about to come up with. My father does not apologize, he only explains. He has a responsibility towards all who work for KK industries."

Jake rather thought this declaration of being above simple morality in the cause of good leadership would have appealed to Sir William Carrick-Boyd, but he didn't say so. He gave his response careful thought and said, "Thank your father for letting me hear his point of view."

Mr Kankuro looked darkly suspicious when he heard that translated. A grim downturned smile grew on his face and he got up and came at Jake on light feet. It was almost like an attack move and it came as a shock to find that he was getting a bear-hug from the captain of industry. And another harder hug. Then Mr Kankuro held Jake by the shoulders at arms' length and growled in English, "You are a good boy."

The interview was over. Icky's father gave Jake's shoulders a last shake, let go and went back to pick up and drain his drink before he walked to the door to another room. Here he turned, his English remarkably improved by the whisky.

"We will meet again. Pleasure to know you."

When he opened the door Kate was standing there. Mr Kankuro spoiled the moment by chuckling uproariously. You could still hear it as he went into the room and shut the door on Kate, who had stepped into the drawing room.

She had been allowed to choose her own clothes. Jeans and a soft top. She looked great, if nervous.

"Hi," Jake said.

"Hi."

"You want me to go?" Icky asked in a tone which said he wanted to stay and see this.

"Do what you like," Jake said.

"OK, I'll stay. Listen – you won't be living together, but you'll both be in London, so you can meet and everything – if you want to."

"D'you want to?" Kate asked Jake.

"Yes. I do."

"Me too."

"I really like you, Kate. I mean, *I* like you. Whoever I really am – I like you."

She smiled. "You've said it three times. I get the message."

"Sorry."

"It's OK. I like you too, Jake."

Later they signed the contracts, which were witnessed by Ichimoro Kankuro and the translator. They were allowed a short time together alone, too, before dinner was brought to them, when Icky rejoined them. In that time they did not say much.

Kate asked Jake, "You were trapped with the crazy brother. They told me. But they never said what happened to him."

"He died."

"That makes sense. Since just about everyone else did, too."

"Saves everyone a lot of bother, probably."

"Yes. Probably."

"I liked the brother. Sholto," Jake reflected. "The only one I did like. Billy did it, you know – brought the castle down."

She shuddered. "He was crazy too."

Jake said firmly, "Well, he's dead as well. Forget about him."

Billy Carrick-Boyd was alive and reasonably well.

Very active, anyway.

The greater part of the hybrids' ceremony chamber had survived. Members of a branch of the security forces were even now going through it meticulously. Their excavations had been delayed by the need to exterminate every life form within a two-mile radius and only now was it safe to return. The central focus of the area, the bronze altar piece, was not there for examination and they had no knowledge that it had ever existed. Kate's deal with Mr Kankuro had specified that she would not have to endure interrogation about her time at Broomcleuch and she was the only one who could have told them about the artefact.

Which was moving along the land-fault at a depth of two hundred metres and at a distance of some forty kilometres. It formed the head of a curious subterranean procession.

Several thousand crawling cockroaches were at the tail end of the line of creatures that traversed the land out of sight of anyone, moving stealthily beside a shallow underground stream. They were drawn ever onwards as by a magnet or Pied Piper by the thing at the front. Behind that thing came the surviving roach-man hybrids. There were only fifty or so of these and they had been taught a verse from a famous Scottish poem to chant along the way – to keep up their spirits.

Despite his underdeveloped voice-box, the creature with the plier-like hands was singing it now, in his mushy gasp.

"Where the pools are bright and deep
Where the grey trout lies asleep,
Up the river and o'er the lea
That's the way for Billy and me..."

Billy liked the song. It was good for his self-esteem. He rode at the head of the procession on the strong, bronze-speckled back of the twenty-metre cockroach that was, in one sense, his most prized possession and in another, his friend, since it possessed a rudimentary intelligence and had the capacity to experience emotion.

Though her markings were unique she was recognisably of the genus *Blaberus cranifer*, the Death's Head Cockroach, and she carried seven large eggs in the capsule that hung between her hind legs. The other four legs contributed to an uneven, swaying motion that Billy greatly enjoyed.

Her delight was to have Billy on her back.

And her purpose was to survive.